Caroline Plaisted

Piccadilly Press • London

CAROLINE PLAISTED worked in publishing for fourteen years before the birth of her daughter in 1994. Since then she has become a freelance editor and has taken the opportunity to indulge in writing. Caroline lives in Kent. This is her third book for Piccadilly; her other two books are *Enter the Boy-zone: Sport Sorted for Girls* and *Girl Power*.

Printed and bound in Hungary by Interpress for the publishers Piccadilly Press Ltd, 5 Castle Road, London NW1 8PR

A catalogue record for this book is available from the British Library

ISBNs:1 85340 591 4 (trade paperback)

Design by Judith Robertson
Cover design by Isobel Smith

I WANT THEM TO GO "WOW!"

I threw the magazine down on the floor in disgust. I'd just read an article in my favourite magazine *Girl Power* about girls who were prepared to do almost anything in order to get a boy, and had found myself beginning to wonder exactly how I could pinch the gorgeous Greg from my best mate Ruth.

"Good grief, Cassie," I said to myself as I looked at my spotty face in the mirror next to my bed, "no bloke's worth losing your best friend for."

I contemplated a couple of the zits on my chin and poked at them with my fingers. Why is it that you can do everything exactly right and still get acne? I hadn't eaten any chocolate bars for weeks – well, at least one week, anyway. I'd cleansed, exfoliated and toned my skin until I was, almost literally, blue in the face. I'd slapped on the Blitzzit cream that *Girl Power* had raved about in the last two issues. And *still* I had a face that astronauts would be proud to land on and explore. To make things even worse, my dear old mother kept on telling me in pious tones, "But, darling, you never *had* spots until you started using all those lotions and potions on your face. I'm sure they are only making things worse." Oh yes? And what would she know about it? When was the last time she'd read a magazine aimed at dynamic girls of my age?

A dynamic girl. That's what I wanted to be – dynamic. If I was dynamic then I'd know exactly what outfit to wear and when. The boys would be positively salivating at my sapphire-blue painted toes. All the girls would want me to be the guest of honour at their parties. If I was dynamic then I wouldn't have a spotty face, non-designer jeans, and be wondering whether I should be saving for an orange hooded fleece or a silver bubble jacket. If I was dynamic, I wouldn't be sitting on my own in my bedroom on a Saturday morning contemplating my zits . . .

"Cassie! Cassie darling!"

I was just preparing myself to not resist the temptation of squeezing the biggest of the two spots on my chin when Mum yelled up the stairs.

"Cassie! Are you there?"

Honestly, of course my mother knew I was there. Where else did she think I'd gone since she saw me slumping up the stairs after breakfast? Down the drainpipe to head for the MTV studio to present my latest show?

I opened my bedroom door just a wincey bit and peered out. "Yeah?" I snarled, in what I hoped was the Attitude I needed to be dynamic.

"Cassie, I've just made some fresh coffee. Come down and have some before I go off to the studio for class." My mum was smiling at me through the door, oblivious to my attempts at dynamism, and trying to get a peek at my room by straining to look over the top of my head. Boy, can she be a pain at times! She just hates me buying magazines ("Such a waste of money, darling,") and is always looking for an excuse to tell me to chuck my old ones out. She just doesn't understand that all those back copies of *Wow* and *Cool* could well hold the key to my future success in the world.

I slipped out of my room and slammed my bedroom door shut behind me. "I shouldn't really have coffee you know, Mum. All those toxins and the caffeine is bad for the lymphatic system."

I tried to walk elegantly down the stairs behind her – the way I'd read about in one of my mags. Then I caught the toe of my trainers on the bottom stair and went crashing into my mum as she headed into the kitchen. Not exactly cool.

"Are you all right, dear?" Mum said.

"Course I am!" My cheeks were about to explode with the heat of my blushing. Rats. I knew if I'd bought KangaRoos instead of these cheaper things I'd be better off. More stylish. More cool.

Mum handed me a mug of coffee. "Did Dad tell you that Ella's coming home for a few days next week?"

Ella's my big sister. She's a model and dead attractive and glamorous. So she's a dead pain to have for a big sister. Well, can you imagine it? Think about it:

1 She's tall.

2 She's skinny.

3 She's got long legs.

4 She's got great clothes.

5 She's got terrific shoes.

6 She's got all these great blokes desperate to go out with her.

7 She's survived being a teenager and has just had her twentieth birthday.

8 She's been on the telly more than once.

9 She can speak French (despite the fact that she failed her GCSE) and a little bit of Italian.

10 She's got her own sports car.

Just about the only thing she hasn't got is a spotty face. As they say: Ain't life a bitch?

Before my skin turned a permanent shade of green, I

came out of my thought-zone and landed firmly back in the kitchen.

"Cassie? Did you hear me? Ella's coming home from Paris next week. Apparently she's got an audition for a cosmetic company in London. It might be a big new contract for her – won't that be great?"

What did I tell you about life being a bitch? Couldn't Ella just be an ordinary model? Oh no, she has to be a supermodel!

"Yeah, great." Well, I supposed I might at least get some of Ella's cast-off make-up when she turned up. And maybe I could angle for some of her 'last season's' clothes, too. Hey – don't get me wrong, though. Ella's OK really. Except when you go to a party and the only reason the boys want to talk to you is because they've heard that your big sis is a model and are wondering if you might be able to introduce them to her some time soon . . .

I slipped my green-tinted specs back into the recesses of my mind just as Mum started to panic.

"Yikes – is that the time?" Mum looked at her Swatch (aren't parents so embarrassing when they try to look trendy?), put her coffee mug in the sink and picked up her gigantic bag. "I've got fifteen four-year-olds in twenty minutes and I've got to pick up Mildred on my way. See you later. Bye, darling!" And Mum disappeared off in her little yellow car that Dad calls her Buzz Box.

You may be wondering what my beloved mother is doing with fifteen four-year-olds and a woman called Mildred on a Saturday morning. You see, dear reader, she's a ballet teacher – and Mildred is her pianist (aged about one hundred and four). So, not only do I have a fabulous-looking big sister but I have a mother who looks good in a tracksuit too. A mother who is fit and forty (ish) and who is sometimes mistaken for another big sister of mine. Aaaagh!

Actually I'd trained to be a dancer for years myself. In fact, I'd got so far with it that I was doing a ballet class after school every day as well as on Saturday mornings. I've done so many ballet exams and competitions since I was about four that I'd stopped being nervous about dancing on the stage. Then one day, about six months ago, I suddenly realised I'd had enough of ballet. All those bashed up toes and aching muscles. All that endless trekking backwards and forwards to lessons with three different teachers (as well, I might add, as my mother) and then having to start my homework at eight thirty every night. So I'd suddenly told my mum that I didn't want to dance any more. Of course, she was more than a bit taken by surprise. But I have to admit she was completely cool about it. "OK," she said, "if that's what you want."

It was my ballet teachers who made me feel bad. They went on and on at my mum about "wasting my talent" and stuff. They thought I was good and should be a professional dancer. What they didn't seem to realise was that I just didn't find it fun any more.

But then, you see, all my ballet teachers know about my family background. I don't just mean about my mum being a ballet teacher, there's my dad as well. I bet you can't guess in a million years what he does for a living. You give up? OK. Well, he works in one of the big theatres in London – he's some kind of director, which means he mixes with actors and dancers all the time. Dad and Mum are always going along to trendy after-the-show parties and meeting people who are in soap operas and stuff. Sometimes they even bring famous people back home for supper. Yes, I'm sure it does sound great. But would you want to meet some gorgeous bloke from the telly on the first day of your first ever period when you've got a zit the size of a double-decker bus on the end of your nose? Have some sympathy for me!

With a family like mine, I should have some dignity and be a *serious* teenager: a kind of modern-day female Sid Vicious who's a rebel *with* a cause. Or something. Instead, I'm a self-conscious almost-sixteen-year-old (I've got about a month to go) who's never taken drugs (not even a puff on a cigarette), can't drink without making a fool of myself (I giggle a lot), and I've never even had a boyfriend, let alone done *IT*. Tell me, what am I doing wrong?

I pondered on this as I dumped my coffee mug in the sink next to Mum's, put on the Marigolds and started to wash up. Then an alarm-bell started to ring inside my head. This was a sad situation: it was a Saturday morning and I was standing at the kitchen sink doing the washing-up. For goodness' sake, nobody had even *asked* me to do the washing-up. And furthermore and notwithstanding, we've got a dishwasher! I felt disgusted with myself. Get real, Cassie. *Get a life!*

There was only one thing for it: to head for Ruth's house to look for some action. And the first piece of action Ruth could help me with was the outfit I'd bought just in case I was invited to Tiffany Green's sixteenth birthday party. Tiffany is so cool she almost lets off a smokescreen of dry ice. She's got great hair, great clothes, great . . . well, everything really. So she was bound to have a great party too. OK – so I hadn't definitely been invited to her party but I was hoping. Which was why I'd spent a lot of my long-saved cash on a pair of really neat cropped trousers and a cute little crop top.

So I rushed upstairs, did a quick change and then slipped into my mum and dad's room so that I could scru-tinise my image in their full-length mirror. Hmmm. I twisted round so that I could take a peek at my bottom. At least there was no visible panty line but my thighs were bulging a bit. I pulled the crop top down to see if I could make it meet the waistband of my trousers. I wasn't at all sure about showing off my midriff to the world. But *Clothes World* (another of my favourite mags, which is essential because it has all the info on cool gear) said it was the latest, so I had to give it a whirl, didn't I? Oh, well, here goes.

I grabbed my coat (a denim jacket that I wasn't entirely convinced didn't make my bum look big), stomped down the stairs, went out of the door and headed for Ruth's house. If there was action to be found anywhere on a March Saturday morning it was at Ruth's. At least she had two older brothers – who might have some good-looking friends . . .

CHAPTER TWO

COME INSIDE – WE'VE GOT TO TALK

One of the good things about my life is that my mate Ruth lives only a few streets away. But her house is so different to mine that it could be a world away. The thing is that Ruth's parents are so cool they are almost scary. My mum is so house-proud that she vacuums under your feet while you are on the loo (it's *true* unfortunately – I know because she did it to me once!), but Ruth's mum says she follows the rule of BTS – Bits That Show. So there's no going on and on about the state of Ruth's bedroom and no hysteria about emptying the bins and stuff.

Ruth's mum is a community midwife so she works unusual hours including some weekends. Her dad is a fireman so he works shifts as well – which, of course, means that Ruth and her two older brothers, Sam and Ben, very often have the house to themselves after school and during the holidays. Can you imagine that? No one telling you to clear up the coffee mugs that are growing hairy stuff under the bed. No one asking you "What happened at school today, darling?". No one to nag that you are spending too long in the bathroom when you should be revising for your GCSEs and to ask you what that blue cream is doing plastered all over your face.

I turned in to Ruth's road and immediately broke into a cold sweat. The house next door to Ruth's was having a roof extension and was surrounded by scaffolding and builders who were all showing off their bum cleavage. Now don't get me wrong: I'm not so desperate that I could fancy a bloke with wobbly buttocks who smells of BO. But don't you just hate the way that even the most disgusting of men reckon that they have a right to whistle and jeer at girls and clearly think that we are going to fall and swoon at their smelly feet? As I tried to saunter past these nasty specimens, so their chanting started.

"Hello, sweetheart! Hey, Barry, take a look at her belly-button!"

I tugged at my crop top fiercely. Oh boy – I could feel my cheeks starting to burn. In fact they were burning so much that you could have cooked a barbecue on them. How I hated those blokes for making me feel so bad and so self-conscious. Why had I decided to wear this stupid top? I hated myself for not being able to ignore those ignorant builders – and then hated myself even more when I tripped up on one of the paving stones and made a complete fool of myself. I didn't so much trip as go splat into Ruth's front gate – which unfortunately was open and so my body seemed to take on its own momentum. (OK, yes, I admit it. These fake Roos with platform soles I'd bought were a disaster. And didn't my dad just love reminding me of that.) One of my feet landed hard on a drain cover and I almost landed face first on the front step – just as the gorgeous Greg opened the door.

"Hi, Cassie," Greg gave me a strange look. Clearly he was puzzled as to why I was planning to knock on the door whilst trying to do a handstand. "Ruth's just gone up to her room. And I'm off to play football at college. See you, Cass."

Greg waited politely while I picked myself up and listened to the humiliating sound of next door's builders laughing explosively at my stupidity. What was worse, I knew that they were probably killing themselves laughing because they thought that I had lost my concentration simply because I fancied them so much. Aaaagh, men! Those with brains are probably OK, but it's those with testicles I'm just not so sure of.

Greg sauntered off, whistling, and I stepped into the house and closed the front door.

"Hey, Ruuth! It's Cassie!" I rushed up the stairs and stormed into Ruth's room. It was absolutely great inside. Ruth's parents had let her decorate it exactly as she had wanted to, so she had fake zebra fur curtains and purple walls and all the window frames and woodwork were painted black. Ruth had got her inspiration from a telly programme – and it was just the sort of room that would make my mum and dad throw a complete wobbly. Well, maybe my dad would be able to handle it a bit better but my mum is definitely into white space and minimalism – which basically means that she wants everything brilliant-white clean and shoved away into a cupboard or preferably into a binbag and taken off to the council dump. Ho hum.

"Hi, babe." Ruth looked up at me from her bedroom floor. She was sitting in a yoga position. Yoga was the latest thing that she was into. "I'm trying to find my inner self," Ruth explained. "Apparently unlocking my inner self will reveal my inner beauty."

Now she was breathing deeply through her nose and exhaling out of her mouth. I know she's my best friend (we've been mates since we were about five), but if you ask me, she looked like a dragon and not a particularly beautiful one either.

I slumped down on Ruth's bed and picked up her latest issue of *Wow* magazine.

"Hey, Ruth – have you read this yet? The article about

snogging? 'The six best snogs you've just gotta have'." I frantically flicked through the pages to see what they had to say. At least if I read about it, I'd be ready for the snog when I got there.

"Nope, I haven't seen it yet. *Wow* only arrived this morning." Ruth untangled herself from her yoga and came to sit with me.

I started to read the article out loud: "SNOG ONE. *Every self-respecting babe has got to have at least one snog on the back seat of a bus before she's eighteen. But choose your boy carefully: you certainly don't want to snog someone who suffers from travel sickness!*"

I stopped abruptly and looked at Ruth who said, "Yuck! That's just totally foul! And so tacky."

"Yeah, but . . . perhaps it depends on the bloke." I was trying to imagine myself canoodling on the bus with a movie star. Mmmm, not so bad.

"Grief, Cass!" Ruth awoke me from my dream. "Get real! No one can be that desperate that they would snog someone on the bus just because that's what it says in a magazine! Sure, if you're with someone nice – just *happen* to be with them – maybe. But do you really want to snog in public? On a *bus?*"

"OK, OK. I get your drift," I closed the magazine and tossed it towards the big pile of other magazines on the floor. Of course I wasn't desperate, I told myself – but I decided to get my own copy of the magazine to read later. Perhaps the rest of the article would actually tell me what snogging was. You know, what you actually do. With your tongue. Things like that. Like how do you actually breathe? That sort of stuff.

"Well, then, what's happening in your life, Cass? What's new?" Ruth was lying down on her bed now and staring up at the amazing ceiling she'd put glow-in-the-dark stars on.

"Mum told me this morning that the prodigal daughter is returning for a few days' holiday. I'm not exactly sure when she is due back but it's some time next week," I rolled my eyes sarcastically.

"Hey – Ella hasn't come home for ages, has she? What brings her away from the fashion world in Paris?" Why is it that everyone – even my mate Ruth – is so impressed by me having a sister who's a fashion model?

"Not for three or four months – in fact, since before Christmas. Mum told me this morning. Apparently she's coming over to do an audition for a cosmetic company, but I don't know which one. God. Can you imagine if she gets it? I expect her face will be in every magazine and on every bus shelter in London. There'll be no getting away from her!"

"*Miiiaaooooow!*" Ruth sat bolt upright on the bed. "Ella's got a great face and an amazing body. I wouldn't mind having a big sister like that who could give me a few expert tips free of charge."

"That's what everyone says! But they don't have to live with parents who go on and on about how 'Ella can do this' and 'Ella does that' and 'Why don't you ask Ella how to do your hair?'. It's as if I'm not allowed to be myself – just a younger version of her!"

I could feel myself beginning to flush again. "Do you know that when I bought this top, all that my mum could say when I showed it to her was, 'Ella would look wonderful in that.' I felt like saying, 'Thanks a lot, Mum, but I actually bought it because I wanted to look wonderful in it myself.' "

"OK, OK, point taken. But don't forget that Ella didn't look anything spectacular at school. It was only when that scout from the model agency spotted her at that fashion show at college and took her along to have her hair practically shaved off that the dazzling beauty emerged. By the way, your top looks good."

Ruth was quiet for a minute while she waited for my temper to die down. She knows I always get a bit over the top just before my big sis comes home to visit. I really wish that I didn't but, you see, I never got on very well with Ella when she lived at home. We were always fighting over something so I was quite glad to see the back of her when she first went to Paris to start modelling. Mind you, I don't

18

think it would be so bad when she comes home if Mum gave me the chance to be with her on my own – but she does have to keep interfering and popping into the room: "What are you two girls up to in here? Why don't you come down to the living-room and sit with me?" That sort of stuff. So it doesn't give me much of a chance to try to get on with Ella, does it?

I picked at a reddish-brown stain that I suddenly spotted on the leg of my trousers. It looked suspiciously like the concrete that the ghastly builders next door were mixing up. Terrific – that was all I needed.

"So, BF," BF is one of Ruth's nicknames for me: it stands for Best Friend, "what fantastical fun-packed evening have you got in store for tonight?"

"Well, I was thinking about phoning up the latest James Bond star. Thought I might offer to show him the sights of this dazzling city of London that we live in and stagger him with my wit, charm and beauty – you know the sort of thing. But then I had second thoughts – after all, he is a bit old for me."

"So in other words you're not doing anything." Ruth had started to paint her toenails a neon green colour. "Tell you what, why don't you come out with me and Greg? We're going to the sports centre to watch a game of basketball. There's some team visiting from another school to play Greg and Ben's college. Should be some talent there,

I reckon." Ruth's eldest brother Ben is at the same college as Greg. In fact it was because he was Ben's mate that she met Greg in the first place.

"OK – you're on. What time?" I'd do anything to get out on a Saturday night. The thought of staying in to watch yet another police drama with my parents was just too much. I'm nearly sixteen, for heaven's sake – I deserve a life!

"Say we pick you up at about seven? The game starts at seven forty-five so we'd have plenty of time to check out the teams before they start all their slam-dunking. We could have a burger after the game. I think Sam and Ben will be there as well. OK?" Ruth was now twiddling her toes to dry the varnish.

"Sounds OK to me." Then I caught sight of the pustules on my chin. "But I'm not really sure it would be a good thing to be seen in public with these things throbbing away like beacons." I couldn't resist giving them another prod.

"Cass – don't be so ridiculous! There's only two of them, you idiot. Anyway, you can always disguise them with some Coveritall cream. Go on, take the tube that's in my make-up bag."

I went over to Ruth's dressing-table and found the tube. I squeezed some of the cream on to my finger and started to blob it on to my spots.

"Are you sure this works, Ruth?" I wasn't convinced.

"Good grief, Cassie! Give yourself a chance. Do you really think that people care more about your spots than they do about the person who has unfortunately got them? Now, take the cream and get yourself glammed up for tonight."

"OK, OK. I'll take it. But what on earth will I wear?"

"Why don't you wear your new outfit? You look fabulous!"

"But isn't it a bit over-dressy . . . ?" I pulled at the Lycra that was sucking itself round my thighs.

"Cassie, it'll be great . . ." Ruth was clearly beginning to lose her patience with me so I felt that it was probably best to make an exit now.

"OK, listen," I looked at my watch, "I'd better get a move on. I've got that essay still to write for History. Have you done yours?"

"That, my dear, is my job for tomorrow. Today I plan to have fun." Sometimes Ruth was almost too cool for her own good. She was so laid-back about her GCSEs it wasn't always good for her. She quite often delivered her work late. I, on the other hand, couldn't sleep on Saturday nights if I hadn't got to grips with my homework by then. It bugged me if I didn't do it – and it bugged me that I did do it and couldn't be more relaxed about it. I stood up and put my jacket back on as I opened the bedroom door.

"See you later then, Ruth. Bye."

"Ciao, bella!" Ruth blew me a dramatic kiss as I tumbled down the stairs.

Ruth's brother Sam was in the kitchen as I walked past to the front door.

"See you later, Sam!"

"What? When?" Sam came to the door, stirring a mug of soup.

"See you at the basketball game. I'm coming with Ruth and Greg."

"Oh, great. Yeah – Ben's playing in the college team. See you then." Sam gave me a wink as he leaned against the door frame.

You know, Sam, I thought, you could be almost fanciable if you weren't Ruth's brother.

I got to Ruth's front gate and decided that I just couldn't face going past those goons next door again. So I gave my crop top another tug down (it was going to ping if I wasn't careful) and decided to walk the long way round back home. That way I could go into the newsagent's and buy that copy of *Wow*.

Back home, about fifteen minutes later, I was faced with a History essay or reading the article about snogging. What a choice, eh? I'm ashamed to say that the essay won the toss. But I did manage to do a quick read of 'The A to Z of Snogging' before Ruth and her gang arrived to get me that evening. To be honest, I wasn't all that impressed – snogging sounded like it had a lot more to do with tongues and spit than love if you asked me. Yuck!

That night, the sports centre was packed. Our own college team had loads of support because this basketball game was a league one and we were doing quite well this season. But the visitors had brought a lot of their own fans with them too. In fact, there were a few coachloads of them. The place was positively throbbing with highly charged teenagers.

Over by the court, the cheerleaders were strutting their stuff and waggling their pompoms. I really felt that I should disapprove of them – I mean, honestly, what self-respecting girl really wants to cavort around just so that she can make blokes look good? On the other hand, I reluctantly had to admit that the thought of cheerleading was quite appealing to me. Perhaps it was all my ballet training. I looked at all the cheerleaders and realised that I could kick my legs at least as high as them and I was probably more musical and better coordinated to boot. The problem was though, if I got into cheerleading, wouldn't people think I was a twit rather than a girl with Attitude?

Back in our seats, Ruth and Greg were holding hands. They didn't look at all self-conscious or embarrassed – just perfectly natural and comfortable. I dreamed of being that OK with a boy. Some chance. Sam was sitting next to me and he passed me a bag of popcorn.

"Want some, Cassie?" He gave me a smile.

"Sure, thanks." I grabbed a handful and started to chomp away just as the game started.

The noise around the court was incredible. The game was going to be a close one because both teams were good. I could see Ben out there and at one point he gave us a quick wave. Sam and Ruth were really proud of him and cheered like crazy when he had the ball. Greg and I screamed away with the best of them when our team scored a basket. It was good to be having fun and part of the crowd. So good, in fact, that I'd quite forgotten about my spotty chin. At one point, after the first half, Ben got a basket himself. The four of us leaped up from our seats and hugged each other.

"Way to go, Ben!" Ruth screamed. She wasn't at all bothered about what people thought of her. Then suddenly I realised I was hugging Sam and cheering away – yikes! I quickly let go of him and pulled away from his bear hug. Sam looked as self-conscious as I felt. Ruth meantime was just glowing with excitement and Greg pecked her on the cheek affectionately. Dream on, Cassie, I thought.

The score was close at the end of the game, and I'm not ashamed to gloat and tell you that our team won. Natch!

We all zoomed down to the court to congratulate Ben and his mates. It was only when I got down there that I realised I was standing in a zone full of hunky boys. Coo. This was heady stuff and I wasn't at all sure I could cope with it.

"Well done, you guys," Ruth was thumping some of the lads on their backs. I was impressed with the cool way she punched some of them on the forearm. None of them seemed to mind. They just smiled back. Some of them were being congratulated by girls who must have been their girlfriends. Lucky girls.

"Hi, Cass, how are you doing?" Ben smiled at me as his brother gave him a victory salute.

"Fine thanks, Ben. Well done and stuff, you know," I could feel myself blushing. This was crazy – I didn't even fancy the guy!

But I did fancy one of Ben's team-mates. He was rather gorgeous and blond and I'd been watching him during the game. Now he was standing next to Ben and getting ready to go off to the changing-room with him. He gave me a dazzling smile and I could feel my knees crumbling away.

"Well hello." He moved closer to me. "Now, Ben, my man – aren't you going to introduce me? You can't keep all these beautiful girls to yourself, you know!" Beautiful? Was this boy talking about me?

"Sure, Tom – Cassie, this is Tom. Tom, this is Cassie."

"Cassie, I'm charmed to meet you." The scrumptious

Tom took my hand, bent over and kissed it. Oh, wow! Now my face was bright, bright red – and so was my neck.

I didn't even have time to worry about my looks though because, the next thing I knew, plans were being made by everyone to go along to the snack bar in the sports centre as soon as the boys had got changed. Tom gave me another of his gorgeous smiles.

"Cassie, sweetie. I look forward to seeing you there and getting to know you better."

Oh my word. Had I died and gone to heaven?

CHAPTER THREE

THE
HOTTEST
TOTTY
IN
TOWN

By the time I got to the snack bar I was in a state of panic. Should I go to the loo and check whether the Coveritall was working properly or should I stay in the snack bar waiting for Tom? Ruth picked up on my mood straight away.

"What's the problem, Cass?"

"Grief, Ruth! Did you see that gorgeous boy back there? The blond one?" I opened my eyes really wide and rolled them dramatically.

"What, Tom? He's one of Ben's mates. What's so special about him?" Ruth seemed surprised at my interest.

"He says he wants to get to know me better after the game! What should I do?" The more I panicked, the more my voice got higher and higher.

"Cass! You do what you want! If you want to get to know him, then fine. If you don't want to, then tell him to buzz off. Now, Greg's going to get some drinks in – do you want Coke or a cappuccino?"

"Umm," I couldn't even make a decision about what I wanted to have to drink. "Er, cappuccino, please."

Ruth went off to tell Greg what to order and I was left on my own to panic solo. Should I be witty? Intellectual? Silent and stunning? I frantically tried to remember what the magazine article I'd read about chatting with boys had said I should do. Calm – that was it. I was meant to stay calm. (Huh! That was easier said than done.) Look at him – yes, I was meant to look him straight in the eye. (How did you do that without looking as if you were short-sighted?) And talk with a low voice – that was the other thing it had said. But wouldn't I just sound as if I was doing an impersonation of some boy?

Before I had the chance to decide, the snack bar suddenly filled with people. The home team were ready to celebrate their victory along with their fans and the place was suddenly alive with happy people. I was being jostled a bit and got stuck behind some big bloke with BO. He was tall and I couldn't see round him. Damn, now I'd lost Ruth and Greg. And Sam.

"Well, Cassie, I knew I'd find you in here somewhere!" The smooth tones were ringing sweetly in my ear as I felt an arm wrap itself around me. I turned round and found myself frighteningly, and deliciously, close to Tom.

"Uhh," I was squeaking – pull yourself together, Cassie! – "Hello! Er, hi!" My cheeks were going red again. Aagh! This was not cool.

"Are you hot in here, Cassie?" Tom brushed his hand gently along my cheek. I thought I was going to faint. Was this really happening to me? "Shall we go over to a table by the window?"

Before I had a chance to squeak another reply, I heard Ruth yelling at me. "Hey! Cass! We're over here!" Ruth was gesturing to a table that she and the others had bagged. Now what should I do? Should I go over there or stay where I was with the delicious Tom? So many decisions – why wasn't all this fun like they make out it is in the movies? Megan Rye never had this problem in her last film. No – she just got on with things. She knew where she wanted to go and she just went.

"Madam," Tom placed his hand under my elbow, "let me escort you over to the other side of the room." Wow, he was so cool!

Tom led me gently through the crowd and everyone just seemed to get out of his way without him having to ask or anything. Clearly everyone was impressed. Just like I was.

Ruth slid along the bench and let me slip in next to her and Greg. Tom sat on the opposite bench next to Sam and

Ben. Fortunately, everyone immediately started to talk about the basketball game so I was able to join in with a few 'absolutely's and 'definitely's without having to worry too much about making a fool of myself. In between times, I took sips of my cappuccino which was really too hot to do anything else with.

The four boys got into a heated discussion about some of the tactics of the game. I didn't really know anything about basketball so I quickly lost the thread of the conversation. So did Ruth and she started to chat to me quietly instead.

"Hmm, Cass," she winked at me as she whispered. "Looks like you've pulled there."

"Ruuuth," I gave her a playful tap on the arm. "Shhh! He'll hear!" I looked across the table and fortunately he hadn't: the boys were still animated, talking about the game. "D'you think I have? He seems quite interested – but he's so good-looking!"

"So what? So are you, if you only admitted it. Except, of course, when you've got the froth from your cappuccino round your mouth!"

"What!" I screamed and started to scrub at my lips frantically as Tom, Sam, Greg and Ben all looked up from the imaginary basketball court that they had made on the table.

"You girls OK?" Greg asked, smiling at Ruth.

"Absolutely!" I said without conviction and hoping that my speedy reaction hadn't actually smeared my lipstick and the cocoa powder all over my face.

"Now, you guys." Ruth had all four of them captive in her glare. "I think it's about time you stopped talking about your balls or baskets or whatever it is you call them and started to talk to us."

"Sorry, sis." Sam folded his arms and looked across the table. "You're right. What are you two talking about?"

"Lipstick and boys, I'll bet!" Tom laughed at his own joke.

Ruth gave him one of her most steely glares. "No, actually, we're talking about politics. Why do you think the leader of the Opposition isn't actually the Prime Minister?"

Tom was taken by surprise – he clearly wasn't sure if Ruth was joking or not. Nor, in fact, was I – after all, we *were* talking about boys before I was frantically trying to remove my lipstick of coffee froth.

Fortunately, Greg broke the tension when he began to talk about the latest film he'd seen with Ruth. The rest of the evening passed quickly – we seemed to talk about loads of stuff. After a while even I stopped being tongue-tied and was able to chat away with the rest of them without feeling too self-conscious. Good job, I thought, that I'd read that article about making small talk on your first date. Except this wasn't my first date, was it? This was just a chat with some mates, some of whom happened to be boys.

Just before ten o'clock I realised that I ought to be heading for home, otherwise my mum would have a fit. Mum was paranoid about my safety. "Cassie, darling – we live in London," she would say. "None of us have a clue about how many monsters there are out there." Honestly, mothers!

I caught Ruth's eye and tapped meaningfully at my watch. She got the hint straight away. "Sorry, you guys, but we girls have got to be going. Are you going to walk us home?" Ruth was looking at her big brothers.

"Course." Sam got up and put on his jacket and Ben started to do the same.

Tom slid out from the bench and helped me to put on my jacket. "It's been good meeting you, Cassie. Perhaps we could meet up again some time?"

"Yes, pl –" I tried to stop myself from looking desperate. Now what would Megan Rye do now? She always had the most perfect flippant remark to make. One that sounded like she was interested but not that interested. One that sounded cool. So I looked Tom straight in the eyes.

"Yes, that would be nice." Nice? Why did I have to use such a pathetic word as nice?

"Yes." I was grinning like some kind of nincompoop.

"Bye, Tom." Ben and Greg thumped their college friend on the back.

"Bye, you guys, Ruth. Bye, Cassie." Tom waved at us as he headed over to join another group of college students.

I noticed some rather pretty girls amongst them. Oh well, I thought, it had been too good to be true.

Ruth and the boys followed behind me. Then suddenly I remembered an article I'd read in *Girl Power* magazine: *As you go, remember to turn round and give the hunk one of your winning smiles and a little wave.* I thought no further and turned. I caught one of my shoes with the other one and crashed into Ruth, who in turn got knocked backwards into Sam and Ben and Greg.

"Hey, Cass. Are you all right? What happened?" Ruth pulled me back up. I was blushing furiously.

"Oh nothing. I just tripped. Let's go." I almost flew out of the café. Oh good grief. Do you think he saw me?

We walked home, Greg and Ruth arm-in-arm and me walking between Sam and Ben behind them. When we got to my house, Ruth held back from the boys and had a quick chat with me.

"I'll catch up with you at school, Cass. I'd better not have any distractions tomorrow because I haven't started that History thing yet."

"OK. And thanks for taking me with you tonight."

"No problem. See you, Cass."

"Night everyone!" I called out to the three boys as Ruth caught up with them. Then I slipped my key into the lock and took a deep breath as I prepared myself for the grilling my mum was about to give me about who I'd been with and what we'd been talking about all evening, "After all, it is quite late, dear." Ho hum.

Much later, I lay in my bed looking at the patterns the brightness of the moon was making on my bedroom walls. I was thinking about my evening at the sports centre. Tom really was quite a catch and he did seem more than a little bit interested in me. Still, he hadn't asked me for my telephone number, had he? Never mind.

Another two hours later, I was frantically thumbing through the pages of a magazine by torchlight. I knew that my mum would go bonkers if she saw my light go on – and probably come running in to see if I was all right. Not what I wanted. At last I found it. I knew it was there – an article about asking boys out for a date. Would I dare?

It was the Tuesday after the basketball game. During break, Ruth and I took the first opportunity we'd had to catch up on events since Saturday.

"Personally I reckon the coach from the away team was better-looking than any of his players." Ruth took a swig from her can of Diet Coke and then offered it to me.

"No thanks." I was leaning against my locker trying to remember what the guy in question looked like.

"So, reveal all. Did you get a call from Tom?" Ruth stood up straight and looked at me intently.

"No," I pulled a face. "Nothing." I tried not to look as disappointed as I felt.

"His loss, Cassie. Anyway, it was only a couple of days ago. And you may be interested to know that he did ask Greg for your number. So I gave it to Greg."

"You did?" Hmm, perhaps I wouldn't have to resort to asking Tom out after all. Suddenly though, I felt a bit sick. Supposing Tom rang and spoke to my mum or dad? Oh my God. I think I'd die . . .

CHAPTER FOUR

RUTH
– I THINK
I OWE
YOU
ONE

We had PE after break and both of us started to get our gear out of the lockers. Unfortunately it wasn't raining so we knew that we were destined for a game of netball despite the freezing cold wind that was swirling around the building. Yummy. I couldn't wait.

As we set off for the PE block, Ruth started to talk about her plans for the holidays. We finished school on Thursday for the Easter holidays and our GCSEs started next term.

"I've decided I'm definitely going to go for it. I checked with my mum and she didn't seem bothered – mind you, she was in a rush to get off to work at the time. Neat move, eh?"

"I'm sure I'd agree with you if I knew just exactly

what you were talking about. What is it that you are going to go for?"

"Some body piercing! I've decided to get a belly-ring!"

"You what? And your mum actually agreed? I don't believe it!" I was impressed – and not just at Ruth's ability to persuade her mother. I hadn't yet got round to having my ears pierced. The thought of attaching a ring to my navel made me feel quite wobbly. "So where are you going to get that done, then?"

Ruth opened the doors into the changing-room. "Thought I'd go along to Oxford Street on Friday. Fancy coming with me? You could have yours done too."

"You're kidding, aren't you? Can you imagine my mother agreeing to that? I haven't even persuaded her to let me have my ears pierced yet! She's said I'll have to wait for my eighteenth birthday before I can do it!" Yet another example of my mum being so sensible about things – she hadn't even let Ella get away with it. Was it any wonder that I was such a goody-two-shoes myself?

"Come with me anyway. We could spend the day doing the shops. Revision can wait until next week." It was typical of Ruth to sound like she couldn't care less about schoolwork, but then she was lucky enough to have an almost photographic memory. And lucky enough to have a rather sharp brain to go with it. This girl will go far.

"OK, then. I might find the jacket I need when we're there."

"Great stuff. Now then, let's hit that netball court!"

We finished school early on Thursday (still no contact from Tom) so Ruth came back with me for coffee. As usual for a Thursday, my mum was at home.

"Ruth, sweetheart, how are you?" Mum was at the door almost before the key was out of the lock.

"Fine thanks, Mrs Lang. How's things?" Mum thought that Ruth was great and never had a bad thing to say about her – at least I didn't get grief about my best friend.

"Pretty good, I think, Ruth. Did Cassie tell you that Ella's coming back early next week?" Mum had a sickly sweet smile of adoration on her face.

Aaagh! Was there no stopping this woman's pride in her eldest daughter? "Put the rose-coloured specs away!" I muttered a little too loudly as I headed for the kitchen and switched the kettle on.

"Sorry, darling? What was that you said?"

"Oh, I just wondered if you wanted a cup of coffee, Mum." I could feel myself flushing pink.

"No thanks. Actually I've just had one and I'm off to meet your father at the theatre. It's the first night of the new production – it's such a shame that you didn't want to come with me, Cassie."

To be honest, I'd had enough of all the luvvies in theatre-land for the moment. Before I had the chance to comment, Ruth played an ace and got me out of having to make excuses for myself.

"I need to go to Oxford Street tomorrow, Mrs Lang. You wouldn't mind if Cassie came with me, would you?" Ruth gave the sweetest of her smiles and Mum melted in front of her. It was sickening!

"Oh no. Not at all. Are you going to buy something special?" Mum returned Ruth's tooth-flasher.

"Actually I'm going to have a ring put in my navel, Mrs Lang." The smile was still there but my mother's crumbled for a second and then, half-heartedly, reappeared.

"I'm sorry, dear? Your navel?"

"Yes, my mum has said I can go ahead and get it done so long as I pay for it and make sure that it doesn't go septic. But being a midwife, she's a bit of a belly-button specialist, so to speak. So not much chance of it going all gooey, is there?" Ruth's teeth were sparkling under the kitchen spotlights. "Cassie must have told you how desperate she is to have her ears pierced, Mrs Lang, hasn't she? I had mine done years ago and I've never had any problems. Why don't you let Cassie have them done too? They'd look fantastic on her, honest they would. Some nice plain gold studs would look great."

Mum was speechless. I think she was still contemplating

the thought of a gooey, septic belly-button – she looked a bit green. "Um, well, I did say to Cassie that she really ought to wait until she was eighteen."

"Oh, Mum. Everyone at school has got at least their ears pierced! One girl in the sixth form has got six hoops in one ear alone! Even your ears are pierced!" At this rate I was going to go into the record books as being the only girl in London over the age of twelve without pierced ears.

"Well, Cassie. I really don't know . . ." Mum looked at me. "Well . . . I suppose . . . well . . . if you had them pierced in a *proper* place. You know, a *clean* place. I expect Ruth knows somewhere like that, don't you?"

I could not believe it. Every other conversation I'd had with Mum about this had ended with me slamming doors and huffing and puffing all over the place while my mother steamed downstairs. It certainly hadn't ended with me being allowed to have my ears pierced!

But Ruth was taking the whole thing in her stride and was avoiding making eye contact with me. She obviously realised that she had my mum wrapped around her little finger.

"Of course, Mrs Lang. I was thinking of going to one of the large department stores. Perhaps Selfridges. They only use sterile equipment and pure gold studs and hoops."

"Yes. Umm . . ." I think Mum was as surprised with herself as I was. Perhaps it was just the relief that I was only asking for my ears to be pierced and not some other, more delicate part of my body. Whatever, she was being charmed by Ruth. "Yes, well, I don't know." Mum was beginning to get strong again and started to shake her head. "I can't help thinking you should wait a couple more years. At least until you've left school."

"I knew it." I plonked my coffee cup down on the work surface in disgust. "At this rate, I'll have to resort to asking one of the girls at school to pierce my ears in secret."

Now my mum really did look worried. "Oh, Cassie, you wouldn't, would you? Imagine the lack of hygiene! Oh no. It's just not worth it." She put her hand to her mouth.

Ruth immediately took the moment to start her smarm technique again. "That's precisely why it would be best for Cassie to come and have her ears done with me, Mrs Lang. I'll make sure she has them pierced properly." Her face was serious and innocent.

"Well. Perhaps . . . Maybe . . . I'm sure that a respectable department store would do it properly. But, I'm still not entirely convinced."

"But what harm would a pair of plain gold studs be, Mrs Lang?" Ruth was seizing the moment.

"And I'm not even asking for you to pay for it. I've still got some money left over from Christmas." Grief – did admitting I still had cash left over after nearly four months make me sound like a total pencil case?

"Oh, all right. I suppose that you are old enough to cope with them now. But it's up to you to make sure that nothing goes wrong with them, Cassie."

Honestly, she was talking to me as if I was an incompetent two-year-old! But I wasn't going to lose this opportunity.

"Mum, thanks! That's brilliant!" I gave her a hug and a great big peck on the cheek. It was so big that a smacking noise reverberated around the kitchen.

"Ruth, let's go upstairs. I've got a magazine that's got the most fantastic feature on body-painting in India." I could see my mum beginning to look a little bit faint. She obviously thought that earrings would be the beginning of the end of her well-behaved little girl. "Have a great time at the theatre, Mum. See you later."

Upstairs, Ruth slumped into the old armchair that I had rescued from my gran's house. I'd covered it with a shawl I'd found in a junk shop. Mum *hated* it and thought that it must be simply covered in fleas and nastiness. Definitely not clinically correct.

"Ruth, I owe you one. You were just great down there."

"Think nothing of it, sweetie." Ruth picked up the magazine that I'd been talking about. "Anyway, by the time that she finds out you've had your belly-button done, it will be too late for her to do anything about it."

Now it was my turn to go into a faint. "You what? A belly-ring? No – no way. No way!" To say I was shocked was an understatement.

"Oh come on, Cass! Every cool girl is having one done at the moment. It's just the thing to show off during the long, hot summer holiday that's coming up after our exams."

"Well, you can call me an old fart if you like, but I think I'll just start with my ears at the moment, thanks."

To be honest, on top of the horror of having the ring inserted, I couldn't imagine having the courage to show off my stomach to the world at large. I mean, can you imagine standing at the bus stop with your midriff on display?

"You're an old fart, Cass!" Ruth laughed and went back to flicking through the magazine.

"Now," I said, opening my wardrobe, "let's get down to the serious business of deciding what I'm going to wear tomorrow to have my ears pierced . . ."

Later that evening, after Ruth had gone home and my mum had gone to meet my dad at the theatre, I was in my room painting my fingernails and trying to make neon-white patterns on them. Just as I got to the most crucially technical bit, the phone started to ring.

"Damn!" I put the polish down and tried to open my bedroom door without smudging my nails. I wasn't successful.

I answered the phone from my parents' bedroom rather crossly. "Yes? I mean, hello."

"Hello, is that the gorgeous Cassie by any chance?" It was a boy's voice.

"Yes, who is this? Is that you, Greg?"

"No, Cassie, it's Tom. We met at the leisure centre on Saturday."

Reader I almost dropped the phone . . .

CHAPTER FIVE

IT'S NOT JUST MAKE-UP – IT'S AMMUNITION!

I was speechless. Then I tried to speak and it was a great mistake. Instead of a controlled, sexy-sounding tone being sent down the line this weird squeaking noise appeared to be coming from my throat without any input from me. *I* didn't recognise myself so I would have been surprised if Tom did.

"Hi – um – yes. Hi." This was hopeless.

"Is that you, Cassie? Have I got the right number?" With all the squeaking, Tom obviously thought that he had got through to the pigsty at some urban farm.

"Er, no," my mind was sending these messages to my mouth telling it to deny all knowledge so that perhaps the conversation could start again. "Er, yes – it is."

"It is Cassie? Hello – are you there?" Clearly he was about to hang up. I seized the moment.

"Yes, Tom!" Now I was shouting. "Yes, Tom, it's Cassie. How are you?"

"Is there a party going on or something? You're talking very loudly. Anyway, I'm fine now I'm talking to you." Despite the fact that I was acting like some kind of village idiot, I could feel my knees melting all over again. Tom was actually ringing me. *Me.*

"Ooohh." I really was making a fool of myself!

"I really enjoyed talking to you on Saturday, Cassie. I was wondering, would you like to come out with me on Saturday night? I thought perhaps you'd like to come with me to a party? Do you know Tiffany Green? It's her birthday party and I'd love to go with you."

Did I know Tiffany? Of course I did – hadn't I just bought the outfit to go to the party and then suffered the humiliation of not being invited? Still, perhaps if I went with Tom then Tiffany would have to take a bit more notice of me. That would show people if I turned up with the delicious Tom dangling from the end of my arm!

"Yeah, sure. Actually I was going to the party anyway." I tried to sound nonchalant but my brain was wondering why my mouth was telling porkies.

"Well, that's just great! Shall I meet you there at about eight on Saturday?"

"Of course. Yes. See you there, then," and I put down the phone. And then I realised that I'd just cut him off without saying goodbye or anything! Clearly I was a moron. Panic started: I had a date on Saturday night. *My first date.* Oh my word – there was so much to do and I only had two days to get ready!

"Get a grip, Cassie," I told myself as I caught my reflection in the long mirror on my mum's wardrobe door. Two days to blitz those zits, get my hair looking like that girl's in the American comedy show (despite the comments my dad made about her), paint my nails, choose an outfit and, well, everything really.

Somewhere, I knew, in one of my mags, there was an article about getting ready for a date. 'Countdown to love' or something like that, it was called. I set off to find it immediately. This situation was urgent.

After about twenty minutes of searching, I unearthed the copy of *Dynamic* that had the article I was looking for and flopped down on my bed to read it:

COUNTDOWN TO LOVE

So he's finally asked you out for that special date? Well, get cool, get ready – get going, girl, for the night of your life!

THE DAY BEFORE

Sort out the clothes you are going to wear. Wear something that you know you look good in. Wear something that you know doesn't make your bum look big or is two sizes too small or too big. And make sure that you wear the right thing for the right date! If you are going to a sports match you'll probably feel out of place in a micro mini. But if you are going to a restaurant then you probably don't want to wear your glittery shorts either!

If you can't make up your mind, ask your best mate to help you decide on the outfit to knock him dead. But, whatever you do, don't leave the decision until the last moment because it will probably make you panic! Check your dream outfit is clean and ironed – you don't want any last minute disasters when you discover that your top has a huge, unsightly splodge of spaghetti bolognese down the front!

Huh – like I've got so many outfits to choose from that it'll take me hours in the first place! I should be so lucky . . .

THE NIGHT BEFORE

Get your beauty sleep! It may sound like something your great granny would have done but the old girl was right, you know. There's nothing like a full night's kip to make you look better in the morning. Who needs to take eye baggage with them on a date?

I put the magazine down in disgust. How could any girl sleep if she was suffering from nerves? What about all those butterflies zooming round my tummy? I lay back and contemplated the paint on my bedroom ceiling for a while. But then my curiosity overcame my disgust and I picked up the mag again to find out more about what I should be doing. A girl had to be cool about this.

DATE DAY

BREKKIE

Have a proper breakfast – no fasting on a day like this! Top up with some decent calories and it will set you up for the very important day ahead.

AFTER BREAKFAST

Sort out your face. Start by thoroughly cleansing and toning and then slap on a face-mask. Relax while you wait for the mask to do its work, by listening to your favourite CD, or perhaps you could watch a video?

Well all this would be easy – as long as my mum didn't come in to pester me about my face-mask. I sat up and took a look in my bedside mirror (in my experience you just can't have enough mirrors in your house when you've got spots) and had an in-depth study of my face. Would it be possible, I wondered, to find a face-mask that would make all my zits disappear?

Then the magazine went on about washing your hair and doing your make-up – you know, all that sort of stuff. By the time I'd finished reading it I was feeling depressed. Grief – I was going to have to go out and buy a whole new bag full of make-up if I was ever going to be able to make a success of this date. I thought about my bog-standard lip-gloss and my ever-so-ordinary beige eyeshadow and wondered how on earth I was going to be able to make any effect on Tom at all. *Don't forget*, the magazine said, *it's not just make-up, it's ammunition!*

I closed the magazine and placed it on my stomach as I lay on my back. Ammunition. Make-up was ammunition, was it? Well perhaps I'd better get a bit of practice at loading my guns now. Tonight. So I went over to my dressing-table and started to sort through all the make-up I'd got . . .

Two hours later I looked at my reflection in the mirror. Perhaps I'd overdone it on the face glitter front – I looked like one of those cheap Christmas cards you get that are covered with glitter that doesn't really stick to the card. No, I obviously had to be more subtle about this make-up lark. In fact, it might be a good idea to have a word with Ruth about it. She always seemed to get these sort of things right. I looked at my watch. It was gone ten o'clock. Too late to call her now. Still, I was seeing her first thing tomorrow morning anyway, because it was Friday. The day that I was off to get my ears pierced in Oxford Street.

Two hours later still I was lying in bed *trying* to get my

beauty sleep but I just couldn't nod off. My brain was too busy whirring away and worrying about what I was going to wear on Saturday night.

I didn't tell Ruth about Tom's phonecall until we were actually sitting on the bus that was taking us to Oxford Street. By that stage, I knew that there was no way that even my mother's supersonic hearing could reach us.

"Cassie! You old tart!" Ruth shrieked at the top of her voice, making even some of the deaf old ladies turn around. "Actually," – thank goodness she was now whispering conspiratorially so the entire busload didn't have to hear all my intimate details – "I knew he would. Only I didn't say anything – just in case he didn't actually ring. You know." She gave me a playful nudge with her elbow.

"Well he did." That blush was coming up again, I could feel it. "And I'm going to meet him at Tiffany's at about eight."

"What?" Ruth's jaw fell open. Good job she didn't have many fillings or they would all have been on display. "*You* are meeting *him* there? What kind of date is that? Why isn't he coming to meet you at your house and taking you there with him? Cassie, you're a dope!"

I opened my mouth to reply but nothing came out. I couldn't think what to say. After I'd put the phone down on Tom I had wondered a bit about why he wasn't taking me with him. But then I just figured that perhaps that's what you did when you went out with a boy.

"Cassie – Tom drives his own car! It's not exactly difficult for him to take you. I think you should ring him back tonight and ask him to come and collect you." Ruth slumped back into the bus seat looking satisfied with herself, glad that she had come up with a solution to what she obviously saw as a problem.

I was too embarrassed to reply straight away. I sat looking down at my hands, twiddling my thumbs around each other. I opened my mouth to say something and then shut it again. I must have looked like a goldfish. Then I took a deep breath and spoke. But I couldn't bring myself to look up as I whispered, "I can't."

"Can't what?" Ruth was staring straight at me, eyes agog.

"I can't ring him."

"Course you can, Cass! Just ring him and say something like you were wondering if he could pass by your house and pick you up. It won't be difficult. You're only asking for a lift, for heaven's sake." Ruth tutted and looked out of the window. "We're nearly there now."

"Ruth . . . I can't ring him . . . I just can't!" I still couldn't look her in the eye.

"Cassie, I just don't understand. Why ever not?"

"Well, for one thing I don't have his number . . ."

I knew that no self-respecting film star would say such a pathetic thing. But I did.

Ruth interrupted me before I could carry on: "Well I can always get that from Greg. There you are – sorted."

" . . . and for another thing, I couldn't bear it if he came to my house to meet me. After all, would you like it if you were about to go out on your first date and your mother pounced on the poor bloke and interrogated him? I mean, can you imagine my mother? She'd be asking him what size shoes he wears, what his parents do for a living and probably what his intentions are towards her daughter. Tom would be hotfooting it out of the house within seconds, never to be seen darkening my door again. I just couldn't bear it! The date would be over even before it got started . . ."

Ruth stood up and rang the bell for the bus to stop at the next stop. "OK, OK, I take your point about your mother. But you could get Tom to stop outside for you and then just hop into the car and go. Come on, Cass, get a shift on. This is our stop coming up."

We both went to the bus door and waited for it to glide to a halt.

"Honestly, Ruth, I don't think it's a good idea for Tom to come and get me. I'll be nervous enough as it is without knowing that Mum is hanging out of the net curtains trying to get a good look at my date."

The doors hissed open and Ruth and I got off the bus

and headed for the department store.

"You're probably right, Cass. In fact, you're probably better off not even telling her you are going out with Tom anyway. Just tell her you're off to a party with me. It's true, anyway, because Greg and I are going as well now. Tiffany seems to have invited every boy at college but she didn't seem to bank on lots of them bringing their own girl-friends with them. Serves her right for not inviting us in the first place, the old bag!"

We both laughed and pushed open the department store's doors. Once we were inside, Ruth put a comforting arm round my shoulder. "Come on, BF. Let's go and get those lobes of yours pierced."

We had to go up to the third floor to the hairdressing and beauty salon department so we took the escalator up. There was something on every floor that we couldn't resist having a look at. We spent ages playing with a CD-Rom player – in fact, we stayed there for so long that one of the shop assistants came along and stood next to us making "ahem" noises. Then, of course, we couldn't possibly go through the fashion department without fantasising about which outfits we would buy if we had the dosh.

I pounced on a great lace dress that had a dark red shift-thing underneath it. It kind of looked seethrough with-out actually being seethrough. "Hey, Ruth, take a look at this." I held it up against me and looked at my reflection in a mirror. I surprised myself by quite liking what I saw. "Now this I would like to wear to Tiffany's party. What do you reckon, Ruth?"

"Nice one, Cass. If you've got . . ." Ruth looked at the price ticket, ". . . eighty pounds! Cor. Wouldn't it be good to have some disposable income? In fact, wouldn't it be good to have some income at all? Come on, let's get a move on. Third floor, here the dynamic duo come!"

We found the salon easily and walked into the reception area. As usual, Ruth got straight to the point.

"We've come to get some body piercing done, please. Two ears," Ruth pointed to mine, "and one tummy button." She pulled her jumper up a bit and displayed the relevant part of her anatomy.

The woman behind the counter smiled sarcastically and shook her blonde head slowly.

"I'm so sorry, dear, but we don't do any bits of bodies except for ears. So we'll do those for your friend as long as she pays in advance and reads this form before sign-ing it." She gave me another of her smiles and handed me a piece of paper which said lots of things about keep-ing your ears and earrings clean and wiping them with a disinfectant lotion. It virtually said that if I didn't do all these things and my ears dropped off, then it would be

56

all my fault. I began to wonder if my mother had written the form and had snuck it into the shop before I arrived. All the warnings were the things that she had said to me that morning over breakfast.

Meanwhile, Ruth was having a dispute over her navel. "What do you mean, you can't do my stomach? Well, any ideas where I can get it done, then?" Even when she was put out, Ruth still managed to work her charm on people.

The woman leaned over the desk in a conspiratorial fashion and half-whispered to her, "There's a place round the corner in Soho. Go out of the front of the shop, turn left and take the first turning on the left. You'll find the shop at the end of the road – they do tattoos and body piercing. Go there, dear, and they'll sort you out. I gather they are quite safe." Then she started whispering very quietly, "In fact, they did one of the hairdressers here. Of course, if I was younger myself, I might be quite tempted."

"Thanks," Ruth beamed back at her. "Now, let's get Cassie here sorted and then we'll head for Soho. Signed your form and handed over your money, Cass?"

Butterflies were zooming around my own stomach now. I'd wanted to have my ears pierced for years but it had never occurred to me that when the time came I might be the teeniest bit nervous about any pain. Ruth plonked a pen down in front of me and and I picked it up. Should I or shouldn't I go through with it?

The woman behind the counter could obviously tell I was having doubts about my bravery. "Honestly, dear, it really doesn't hurt very much. And it's over in a flash. Rita's the girl who does the ears and she just uses this kind of nutcracker thing and POP, POP, you've got two earrings. Just like that."

"OK, I'll sign." I thought I'd better before I ran out of the store. The words "Doesn't hurt very much" and "nutcracker thing" were ringing in my ears. In fact, I could hear a kind of whistling in my ears anyway.

Before I knew it, Ruth escorted me into a pink-curtained booth where Rita quickly wiped my earlobes with disinfectant and put a blob of biro on each one. She held a mirror up in front of me so that I could inspect the biro marks.

"All right, sweetie? Those in the right place?" Rita had the same smile as her colleague behind the desk.

"Great stuff, Cass." Ruth answered for me because all I could manage was a grunt as I imagined the pain that I was about to be subjected to.

"OK, here goes." Rita got to work. "I just pop the little gold stud in here and," there was indeed a POP, "there you are. Now for the next one," POP, "and you're done. How's that?" She held up the mirror again. I could see the two gold studs sitting embedded in my now scarlet earlobes. I wondered if my ears were in fact throbbing visibly as well as feeling like they were.

58

"Great," I said weakly. "Thanks."

"You OK, Cass?" Ruth was leaning down and staring at me. She looked quite concerned. "Only you've gone a bit pale."

"No, I'm fine, thanks. Come on. Let's go and find your body place in Soho. Thanks, Rita, bye." I stood up quickly and charged out of the beauty salon. I felt the need for fresh air and wanted to get out of the store as quickly as possible.

I must have been walking quite fast because Ruth was trotting along behind me as we zoomed back past the fridge-freezers towards the down escalator. I was vaguely aware of Ruth talking to me but there was suddenly this terrible buzzing in my ears. Then everything seemed to go fuzzy – a bit like a television set that is out of tune. I stopped and turned round to see where the buzz and fuzz were coming from. That's when there was a bang noise, a terrible pain on the back of my head and everything went black.

CHAPTER SIX

RUTH – I THINK YOU OWE ME ONE

The buzzing and fuzzing started up again. Then someone started to tap on my cheek and was shouting my name so that it sounded like it was coming out of a megaphone.

"CASSIEEE! CASSIEEEEE! CAN YOU HEAR MEEEEE?"

I tried to say, "Of course I can, you idiot – do you think I'm deaf?" but as soon as I started to speak I could feel myself wanting to puke. The back of my head was throbbing.

Then everyone started to talk at once. A chair was brought and a glass of water was shoved up my nose. The urge to chuck went away for a bit and I was able to look around me without so much fuzz blocking my view. Ruth seemed to be kneeling down next to me. So did a woman I didn't recognise and all around me were legs of all shapes and sizes.

My head felt like it had been hit with a mallet.

"Fine – only I think I'm going to puke . . ." I started to heave and someone (I don't think it was Ruth) shoved a plastic bowl under my nose. "Where am I?" I looked around and found myself in a sea of fridge-freezers and dishwashers.

"We're still in the store," Ruth said, looking quite concerned about me. "You passed out when we came out of the beauty salon and bashed your head on a freezer as you went down. Pretty dramatic stuff, really." Ruth was looking almost impressed. "All these shop assistants came zooming over and started to faff around you."

A man in a suit suddenly knelt down next to me and grabbed my wrist. Who the heck did he think he was? How dare he grope me in front of everyone! I wrenched my wrist away just as he started to talk to me.

"Are you feeling better, miss? Don't worry. I'm sure you're feeling very disorientated. I'm Mr Berwin, by the way. The first-aider on this floor of the store. If you feel like you could stand up, let's take you into the manager's office. We've got a nice cup of hot, sweet tea waiting there for you. Had a bit of a shock, haven't we? A nice, sweet cup of tea will do you the world of good. Miss Smith?" He gestured at one of the young shop assistants who was standing behind Ruth. "With your help please, Miss Smith, we'll get the young lady to stand up."

Mr Berwin and Miss Smith? Good grief, shouldn't this be the moment in my life when the handsome prince appeared and rescued me? I couldn't see any knights on white chargers. All I had was Mr Berwin and his faithful (female) assistant called Miss Smith. What was cool about this?

With a gentle heave I was on my feet. Something inside my head seemed to roll from side to side – a bit like a marble rolling around in a cup. Perhaps bashing my head had made my brain work loose and that was what was rolling around? There were people all around me, and as we were walking (ever-so-slowly) to the manager's office I could hear some of the things they were saying.

"Drugs, I expect," said one woman sagely.

"Probably drunk. Tsk, tsk." Another one stood there shaking her head.

Ruth suddenly turned round and yelled at the crowd in general, "Look! All the poor girl has done is faint! Had a bit of a shock. That OK with you?" Ruth was good – even in a crisis.

The crowd all stepped back and looked a bit shocked themselves. Then one by one they started to move away and get on with their shopping. After all, choosing a new washing–machine is much more exciting than watching a teenager throw up on a department store's floor.

We got to the manager's office and I sat down in a chair to drink the disgusting cup of tea. Isn't tea such a boring drink? Since when did you see anyone in the more trendy sitcoms drinking tea? No, decaffeinated coffee was much more the sort of thing they had in 'Friends'. I mean, look what happened to the pair in the telly ad for that new brand of coffee: steamy stuff – and I don't just mean the hot coffee!

Now it was Mr Berwin's turn to have a look at the back of my scalp. "I just want to check that there is no open wound," he said cheerfully as if he was delighted at the opportunity of putting all his first-aid skills to the test.

He started to rummage around in my hair and Ruth looked at me sympathetically. "It's OK," she mouthed at me silently and smiled. I finished my cup of tea and put the cup down on the saucer.

"No, nothing there, miss. Still, I think you should take it easy for the afternoon. Shall we get you a taxi to take you home?"

Things were looking up.

"That would be gr– actually, no thanks! We'll be OK on our own!" Ruth had suddenly put a spanner in the works and I just didn't know why. The leading ladies in all the best movies are always jumping into taxis. Now I'd got my chance to (and probably at someone else's expense), Ruth was putting a stop to it before it even had a chance to begin! What was she playing at?

"Are you sure? I think the young lady needs to have a quiet afternoon after her nasty shock." Poor old Mr Berwin hadn't reckoned on the determined Ruth.

"Yeah, of course. But we've just got one more thing to do before we can go home."

One more thing? One more thing better than arriving home in a cab? Was the girl mad? Or rather, was the girl even madder than I thought she was?

"Ruth," I hissed when Mr Berwin turned away to repack his first-aid kit, "what are you talking about?" My eyes were goggling at her but I had to pop them back in a bit because my head was still throbbing.

"We can't go home yet, stupid!" Ruth hissed back. "We've got to go to that place in Soho and get my tummy-ring!"

So that was it. I had completely forgotten that Ruth needed her own bit of body piercing done. Despite all the drama that had happened, and even if I did feel as if my brain had just done three rounds with a boxing world champion, I knew it would be mean to go home now without Ruth's chance of passing out in public.

I took some deep breaths and then stood up. My legs felt a bit jelly-like but otherwise I was OK. "Thanks so much for your help, Mr Berwin." I handed him back his cup and saucer. "Sorry for all the trouble I've caused."

"It's no trouble at all, young lady." Mr Berwin patted

me lightly on the arm. He may have been a great help but I wasn't at all sure that I liked being patronised by him.

"See you later, Mr Berwin." Ruth gave him a wave as she stormed out of the office ahead of me. Clearly Ruth was on a roll and was heading for that belly-ring fast.

"Bye, Mr Berwin. See you." I followed Ruth out of the room.

As I travelled down the escalator I clutched the handrail and suddenly started to feel extremely hot. Phew – I needed to get out into the fresh air. At the end of the first flight, I caught sight of myself in a mirror and there they were – the studs that had started with a fuss and had now ended with a furore worthy of Wyn Patrick, my favourite, most drop-dead-gorgeous-looking film star. I stopped and had a quick peek at them. Well, all right, I admit it. I had a long and lingering peek at them. I had to admit that, apart from a tinge of redness around the lobes, the earrings looked pretty good. Perhaps it had been worth it after all.

IS *THIS* WHAT CINDERELLA WENT THROUGH TO GET TO THE BALL?

Once we'd got out of the store and into the fresh air, I started to feel heaps better. I couldn't for the life of me remember the directions we'd been given in the beauty salon so I just followed Ruth meekly through the maze of streets to the body piercing place. I looked around me at some of the shops as we went along – some of them were just weird and sold all sorts of peculiar stuff. Every now and then we stopped to look in the windows at the really wacky clothes and unbelievably high platforms. But Ruth was in a hurry to get her stomach sorted out and kept on hurrying me up. "We'll go in on our way back," she said.

I just couldn't believe the body piercing place though, when we found it. The windows were almost entirely blacked out, except for a small square of ordinary glass in the middle. We stopped and peered in at it – there were loads of photographs of people with tattoos and rings and studs piercing all sorts of bits of their bodies. Whoa there, I thought. No thank you very much – this is not a place for me.

"Ruth, you simply cannot go in there!"

"What do you mean?" Ruth looked at me, astonished. "This is the place the woman spoke about, I'm sure." She started to head for the door.

"You have to be kidding, Ruth." I got closer to her and started to whisper conspiratorially. "You don't know what they are like. Anything could happen in there, you know. What about hygiene? Ruth, I'm sorry. I simply won't let you go in." I folded my arms and looked at her disapprovingly.

"Oh come off it, Cass!" Ruth's jaw dropped down in disgust at me. "Why shouldn't it be hygienic in there?" She was talking quite loudly and it was embarrassing. People were staring at us as they walked along the pavement.

"Look at the photos in the window!" I hissed. "Look at those people! Weirdos. Some of them have even got rings through their . . ." I could feel myself blushing, "their private bits!"

"Cassie Lang, you sound like your mother! I can't believe you! Why should people be weird and unhygienic just because they have got shaved heads or a tattoo on their shoulder? What's your problem, Cassie? Are you getting suburban in your old age?" Ruth had shoved her hands in her trouser pockets and was looking at me in disgust.

Huh! So I sounded like my mother, did I? Huh! I sniffed and looked away from Ruth. Ouch! To be accused of being like my mum hurt – badly. And Ruth must have known it would. But good grief, I thought, perhaps I did sound like her! Perhaps I was boring! Wyn Patrick wasn't. She would have just gone straight through the door and no messing. Damn, damn, damn. Why was being cool so hard? Damn, damn, damn it!

I think Ruth realised that I was feeling a bit sore about the mother comment. She was looking a bit embarrassed. "Cass . . . I'm sorry."

"It's OK. Come on, Ruth, you're right. Why should people be dirty just because they've got wacky hair or a ring through their nose? Come on – let's go in. Only don't expect me to look!"

"You're a mate, Cass." Ruth gave me a bear hug. "You don't have to look – but I might need you to hold my hand."

We went through the door and a bloke who looked just like the heavy metal rock singers they had way back in the Seventies (the ones our dads talk about) looked up from the black booth that he was sitting in. In the opposite corner, a girl with a million plaits in her hair was having a tattoo that looked a bit like an eagle done on her back. Another girl with jet-black, very short hair was doing the tattoo under a bright spotlight.

"Can I help you chicks?"

Chicks? I couldn't believe him – he even sounded like one of those blokes. Hadn't he actually appeared in one of those Seventies police dramas that they keep repeating on the telly? Ruth started to explain why we'd come and to my horror, from what he was saying, the guy seemed to think that we were both going to have our navels pierced.

"No, not Cassie as well," Ruth said. "Just me, here," she pointed proudly at her flat stomach.

Perhaps, I thought, if my tummy could look that good, I might consider having mine done. But then I realised what I was thinking and decided that I was still obviously feeling very light-headed after all the excitement earlier on.

"Well, doll, let's get on with it." Mr Heavy Metal produced a box from within his black booth and started to fiddle around with rings and needles and stuff.

I shuddered and started to feel dizzy. "Listen, Ruth," I touched her on the shoulder as she started adjusting her top ready for her navel to be changed for life. "Mind if I leave you to it and just take a look at the photos and tattoos?"

"Sure, Cass."

So I had a wander through all the photographs of the different designs that people could have imprinted all over their bodies. I had to admit that some of them were quite good. But imagine if you had a great big spider plonked on your arm and then you went off it a couple of years later! You'd be stuck with it then, wouldn't you? Mind you, a tattoo could be a cool way of making a statement at a party. And there had been a great programme all about body art on the telly the other night. Perhaps if I was going to experiment with some body art myself, I might go in for one of those stick-on transfer tattoos.

My dad would probably go even more ballistic than my mum if he saw a tattoo – even a transfer one. I wondered if I could be that wicked to them . . . but it would be good for a laugh.

"Cass!" I was woken from my thoughts as Ruth came bounding over to me. "Cass – what do you reckon?" She was poking out her stomach at me. She'd done it – there was the famous belly-ring.

"Wey-hey, Ruth. Way to go!" Apart from the redness, it did have a kind of look about it. "It's great."

There was obviously no point in asking her if she was pleased with it. You could tell from Ruth's face that she felt like the cat that had got the cream.

"Did it hurt?" Just the thought of it was hurting me.

"A bit – but I'd have it done again if I needed to! I can't

wait to see Mrs Hunt's face when she sees it!" Ruth was prancing around doing what she thought was an imitation of a belly dancer.

She was right: Mrs Hunt would be as horrified as my mum would be at the sight of Ruth's belly-ring. Mrs Hunt was our headmistress and there wasn't much that she missed. In fact, she was known as Hunt it Out at school. But there wasn't anything she was going to be able to do about the belly-ring as long as Ruth kept it covered up with a plaster during PE. And because of the exams, we weren't going to be having many PE lessons before the end of next term, were we?

"So, Cass," Ruth said. "What shall we do now? Fancy a quick look in that clothes shop we saw?"

"OK," I said, putting my coat back on. "Let's do that. And then I want to pop into the chemist's just along the road for something." Now I'd got thinking about it, perhaps I would have a go at one of those transfers.

We got back to my place late in the afternoon. Fortunately, my mum was out teaching so Ruth and I were able to slouch around in my bedroom in privacy and talk about our adventurous day.

"So – you glad you've finally done it, Cass?" Ruth slurped at her coffee mug.

"You bet. It's just a shame I made such an idiot of

myself." I rubbed the back of my head. "You know, it still hurts a bit now."

"Well I'm not surprised. You went down with quite a whack."

"I still reckon it's a shame though that we couldn't have come back in a cab." I could just imagine the look on our next door neighbour's face: her eyes would have been on stalks.

"Yeah – it would have been good. Never mind, though. We had a laugh. That's why we went, wasn't it?" Ruth nibbled on a biscuit.

"Well yes – but I could have lived without the humiliation bit, you know. Did you hear that woman say I must have been on drugs? The cheek! Do I look like a junkie?" I plonked my own mug down on the dressing-table in disgust.

"Well, not to me, Cassie. But you did look a bit out of it down on the floor next to all those fridge-freezers." Ruth started to laugh and then ducked as the cushion that I hurled in her direction flew towards her head. The rat!

"So, Cass," Ruth put the cushion behind her back and sat with her legs crossed on my bed (I was mildly irritated because she still had her boots on and my Indian bedspread was underneath them. But I tried not to notice). "What are you going to wear for your hot date with Tom tomorrow?"

"I dunno. What do you reckon on my new trousers and that crop top? Will they be OK?"

"You look good in them, Cass. But – and this is a BIG but! You were wearing them last Saturday when you met Tom. You haven't thought about that, have you? Not good, my dear." Ruth rested her hands on her knees.

"Aaaah!" I screamed and leaped to my feet. She was right. I hadn't thought about it. My God. What was I going to do? "Ruth, you have to help me. What'll I do?"

"Let's have a look in that wardrobe." Ruth was up and nosing inside quick as a flash. She'd already helped me with one crisis that day, so perhaps she could bail me out again.

Coat hangers were speeding their way along the wardrobe rail. Every now and then, Ruth pulled one of them out, inspected the garment that was hanging from it and threw it down on my bed. When she'd finished, she turned to the pile of clothes.

"Now, Cass," she put her hands on my shoulders and stood me in front of her, "stand still."

She put a dress up against me. It was one that my mum had given me for Christmas. "No, Ruth. No! I can't wear this – it looks like it's a suction fit on my thighs. No thanks."

"OK." Ruth put it back in the wardrobe and held up a load more things. Between the pair of us, we decided that most of them weren't right for one reason or another.

"What am I going to do, Ruth?" I felt despair. Now Tom would think I didn't have any style.

"Tell you what, Cassie. You could always wear my bootleg jeans with your crop top. Then we could put your tattoo on your stomach and Tom will be so mesmerised with the tattoo on your sumptuous tummy that he won't even notice the top is the same one you wore last week." Ruth was looking very pleased with herself at coming up with a solution to my problem.

"Maybe you're right." I wasn't entirely convinced. But on the other hand, did I really have any choice? It looked like Ruth's bootlegs or nothing.

"Come on, Cass. Don't be defeated. You've got your sassy new earrings for Tom to look at as well as him staring into your fabulous eyes – especially if you put on some decent eye make-up. Now, let's get going on your transfer. Where's the packet?"

"Here," I was rummaging around in my bag, "let's see what it says we have to do."

I read the instructions out loud to Ruth. Clearly, I was going to need her help if I was going to do a decent job with the transfer on my tummy. "Are you sure that my stomach's up to this, Ruth?"

"Sure thing, honey bun." Ruth was repeating one of her mother's favourite phrases. She seemed to say it whatever her kids asked her for. "Now, lie flat on that bed and let's transfer. Which tattoo do you fancy? This spider looks the best to me." Ruth held it up for me to see.

"You're right," I said as I lay down. "Go on then, Ruth. Do it before I change my mind."

I had to try really hard not to laugh as Ruth was doing the tattoo but it didn't take too long and Ruth didn't *quite* loose her rag with me.

When she was finished, I stood up and took a look at the tattoo in the mirror. Then I realised that if I followed the plan from the magazine I was going to have at least two baths before my date so the transfer would probably be gone by tomorrow night anyway! I couldn't get anything right today – and I told Ruth that.

"Well you'll just have to have a shower then, won't you? And don't rub any soap on your stomach." I bet Kate Winslet doesn't have these kinds of stresses. Except of course when she's going down with the Titanic. But even then she looked pretty cool, despite the stress!

Before I had a chance to reply, the front door slammed and my mum came thundering up the stairs. It wasn't like her to be anything other than elegant at all times. There must be something wrong.

"Cassie? Cassie! Are you in?"

There was a knock on the door and I quickly covered up my stomach. I'd let my mum get used to the earrings first before I inflicted the tattoo on her. I opened the door and hoped that my blushing wasn't too obvious.

"Er, hi, Mum. How's things? Is there a problem?" She was in such a state of excitement that she didn't even notice my earrings.

"No, Cassie – oh hello, Ruth dear." Mum smiled at her. Typical that she'd spot her before my throbbing earlobes. "No, I've just got back from the studio. Ella rang me on her mobile – she's on her way from the airport now." Mum was grinning with delight.

"You what? But Ella wasn't due to be in London until next week!"

"Yes, she unexpectedly got an earlier flight. She'll be here in an hour or so, from Heathrow."

"That's great, Mrs Lang." Ruth picked up her bag and her coat and headed for the door. "Listen, Cass, I'd better be going. I'll pop in tomorrow with those bootlegs for you. See you later. Bye, Mrs Lang. Bye, Cass."

"Bye, Ruth – and thanks for your help today." I'd already decided that I wasn't going to mention the fainting incident to my mum in case it made her faint too and never let me out of her sight again.

Wasn't that just absolutely great? Darling Ella was coming home tonight instead of on Monday. Brilliant. Absolutely brilliant. Now I wouldn't even be able to have a first date without her getting in the way.

Absolutely brilliant!

CHAPTER EIGHT

THE
STYLE
COUNCIL

Mum rabbited on for ages, panicking about getting Ella's old room ready on time and whether or not the food that she had planned to cook for our supper was going to be what Ella wanted to eat. I wanted to ask her if it ever occurred to her that I might not want to eat the supper but I thought better of it and helped her make up Ella's bed instead.

It was funny, because Ella's room was still just like a teenager's one: there were posters on the walls; her old collection of snow scenes; even some clothes hanging in her wardrobe. And yet now Ella was a really successful model and you could find her face in magazines all the time. She'd even had features about her in some of the newspapers because she'd made such a success on the Paris catwalks. Mum and Dad kept all of them and sent them to her in Paris where she now lived. Ella had been in France for a year but none of us had been over to see her there. She seemed to be so busy with her work that she never had time for us to visit. So it was a long time since we'd seen each other – we didn't even speak on the phone very often.

Before she'd started her career as a model, Ella was training to be a classical ballet dancer at a college in London. She still lived at home but she was working very hard training so when she was at home, she just slumped around in an exhausted heap either sleeping or sewing ribbons on her endless pairs of ballet shoes. For some reason we got on each other's nerves and we seemed to argue about everything. It drove our parents absolutely nuts because weekends could be like a war zone in our house.

Then, completely out of the blue, Ella got invited to do some dancing at a fashion show. Other girls from her college were doing it as well and they all got to have their hair and make-up done by professionals. And, of course, they got to wear some stunning designer outfits. She was only meant to do one show but there was a talent scout there from one of the top London model agencies who pounced on Ella and invited her to come along to have some photos taken. The next thing we knew, Ella had been signed on with the agency and her face appeared on the cover of a glossy monthly magazine. Mum and Dad weren't at all happy about it at first because they said that Ella was wasting all her ballet talent and the years of expensive training that they'd paid for. But Ella was dead set on becoming a model by then and there didn't seem to be anything that would stop her. She and Mum even had a blazing row one day when Mum told her not to go through with it. "You'll regret it, you know. It'll be a flash in the pan and over in six months – a year at the most. And then you won't be able to go back to the dancing. Give your ballet career a chance first. Get a job in a good ballet company and then, if it doesn't work, perhaps you can go back to the model agency."

It had no effect on Ella because she'd made up her mind. In fact, she was dead rude to Mum. "Yes, that's right, stay and be a mediocre dancer in some foreign ballet company that tours weird towns and cities that no one's ever heard of, let alone wanted to visit. And then, if I'm lucky and don't get an injury, I'll end up in my thirties look-ing for another job to do. Perhaps I could even become a ballet teacher. How thrilling. At least if I can be a suc-cessful model for a year or two, I can earn some seriously decent money which will help me out when I'm too old to model any more."

I think the bit about being a ballet teacher hurt Mum a lot. After all, she'd had a really good career as a dancer which she'd only stopped in order to have Ella and me. And she was a really good teacher – lots of the kids that she taught went on to have some kind of success. In the end, Mum and Dad gave up trying to change Ella's mind and they decided that the best option they had was to help Ella and make sure she was safe from all the dirty old men that they were convinced were waiting to pounce on their darling daughter. And then they found out that the model agency wanted Ella to move to Paris so that she could be on hand for all the European magazines and the catwalk shows. They went into a total panic – but the agency assured them that Ella was safe with them. She certainly seemed to be because her face was everywhere and she hardly ever seemed to take time off from work.

And now the prodigal daughter was returning home (even if it was only for a short time) and Mum and Dad seemed to have forgotten the fact that they had never wanted Ella to go in the first place. I stuffed the duvet into its cover, gave it a good shake and placed it on the bed. I wondered what Ella's flat in Paris looked like. Was it huge and open-plan, like one of those loft apartments that you always saw in films? Or was it in a modern purpose-built block? Perhaps one day I might get the chance to go and visit her there. I could always dream.

Mum rushed in with some towels and placed them on the bed. "Thanks for doing the bed for me, Cassie. There," she surveyed the room, "that looks good. Now, let's go downstairs and get everything ready for supper. Can you lay the table for me, sweetheart?"

"Sure." I started to thunder down the stairs. These days I took them carefully when I had my fake KangaRoos on. I heard a car pull up outside the house and when I got to the hall, I stopped and peeked out of the window. It was Ella, arriving like a film star in a taxi. Typical!

"She's here!" I called up the stairs to Mum who flew down them and was out of the door before I could blink.

"Ella! Ella! Darling! You're here much quicker than we thought. How are you?" Mum was hugging Ella even before she was out of the taxi.

"Hi, Mum, how are you? Like your top." Ella gestured towards Mum's jumper with her head. I felt chuffed because I'd helped Dad to choose it for Christmas.

Ella was looking fantastic. Her skin seemed to glow and she'd grown her hair so it was long, sleek and glossy. She was wearing a really great pair of zebra-print jeans and a black skinny-rib top.

After she paid the taxi driver, Ella and Mum carried her suitcases up the front path and into the house.

"Hi, little sister, how are you doing?" Ella put a seriously smart set of burgundy leather suitcases down in the hall and stared me straight in the eyes. I bristled at the little sister bit but I let it pass.

"Fine thanks, Ella. How about you?" It seemed weird. Here was my big sister, the person who'd been around for ever as far as I was concerned, and I didn't feel as if I knew her any more.

"I'm great, thanks. Fancy helping me to take my stuff up to my bedroom? Come on." Ella was heading up the stairs ahead of me as I gathered up the other bags. Mum picked up Ella's handbag and quickly pushed her way in front of me so that she was next up the stairs behind Ella.

"Did you have a good journey, darling?" Mum was crooning as if Ella was part of the Magi. "Were you on your own? When's the audition?" She was beginning to sound as if she was nagging already.

Now we were in Ella's room again and with the three of us and all the luggage it was crowded to the point of being intimate. Mum dived down to pick up the largest of Ella's cases and put it on the bed to open it. But before she'd managed to undo the strap completely, Ella said, "Mum, I could murder a cup of coffee. Any chance?"

It was immediately obvious that Ella was determined she was not going to be Mum's little girl any more and that she resented Mum behaving as if she was in charge of Ella still. The air was a bit tense and Mum was taken aback by Ella's reaction. It wasn't good. There was a few seconds of silence before I said, "Sure, I'll make it. Want some, Mum?"

"Er, yes. I'll come and help you, Cassie. We'll see you downstairs in a bit, Ella." Mum gently put her arm up and on my shoulder and started to propel me towards the stairs.

When we were in the kitchen, I filled up the kettle and said, "I expect Ella's a bit tired after her journey, don't you?"

"Yes, darling. She does look a bit tired – she's clearly been working very hard." Mum was obviously feeling deflated and I felt a bit sorry for her. After all, she'd been so excited about Ella coming home – perhaps it was dawning on her that this house wasn't Ella's home any more. Perhaps she felt a bit like I did – that she didn't really know Ella so well any more?

In a near-silence we made the coffee and for some reason I put the three mugs on a tray to take them into the living-room. It was almost as if I was trying to impress Ella.

We could hear her upstairs, moving about in her room and opening and closing wardrobe doors and drawers before she went in the bathroom. We heard the loo flush as Mum led the way across the hall, and as I put the tray down on the coffee table, Ella bounced into the room with a load of carrier bags in her hands.

"Phew, that's better. I'm sorted now." She plonked the bags down on the floor and slumped into the sofa, kicking off her shoes. They were a beautiful pair of JP Tod driving shoes. They were in all the magazines and I was wondering if they might fit me . . . "So, tell me all your news!" Ella slurped on her coffee. "How's the dancing school going, Mum?"

"Pretty good, I think." Mum was off, telling Ella all about her students. Of course, Ella knew quite a few of them – some of them had been in her classes and she seemed to be genuinely interested in what they were up to and their successes. But none of it was news to me, because I knew about it already. What I wanted to know was what was in those rather interesting carrier bags. One of them had Christian Dior written on the side!

The pair of them continued to chat away and I just sipped my coffee and occasionally chipped in when Mum couldn't remember a name or something. Then Ella put down her empty mug and said, "Now, present time," with a great smile on her face.

"Oh, darling, how kind!" Mum said it as if she hadn't noticed the goodies that were sitting wrapped on her living-room floor.

"This one's for you, Mum." Ella handed the silver Christian Dior bag over to her.

"Oh my goodness." She dipped her hand inside and drew out a flat, silver cardboard wallet that also had Christian Dior on the side. Slowly – excrutiatingly slowly –

Mum ever-so-carefully peeled open the cardboard and then removed a layer of tissue paper. With a flourish she unfolded the most beautiful silk chiffon scarf. It was exquisite.

"Oh, Ella it's . . . it's . . . it's just divine!" Mum rushed over and gave Ella a kiss. Perhaps this would make up for the difficult moment earlier on.

"Glad you like it, Mum. I thought you would when I saw it in the window – it was your sort of colours and – well, you know how to wear scarves properly and stylishly."

Mum was positively lapping up the compliments as she swished the scarf around her neck and shoulders. Ella was right, though – the scarf really did look good on her.

"Now, we'll save Dad's one until he gets back from work. Will he be back really late tonight?"

"No – he'll be back in time for supper so you can tell all of us your news at the same time."

Ella picked up another black and white bag. It was shiny and gorgeous – and it said Prada on the side! "This one's for you, sis." Ella swung the carrier in my direction. Wow! I'd have been happy with just the carrier bag but I could feel something inside it. I wasn't as patient as Mum so I dived in to see what it was.

"Hey, Ella – it's gorgeous! Look, Mum, look!" I swung my new treasure in front of her. "It's a Prada handbag! The one we saw in that magazine last month!" I couldn't believe my luck. "Thanks, Ella – it's brilliant!"

"Thought you'd like it." Ella looked almost as pleased as I felt. Then it occurred to me: Ella must be earning serious amounts of dosh if she was buying presents like this for other people, let alone for herself! This girl was doing good!

"Now." Ella rummaged through the other bags. She presented us with chocolates, a huge string of garlic that she'd bought in a Paris market, some really runny-looking cheeses and other stuff to eat and drink. All of them looked and smelt scrummy and the three of us took them into the kitchen to find places for them.

"Need any help with the supper, Mum?" Ella gave Mum one of her breathtaking smiles that had made her such a success with the newspaper journalists. "Only I wondered if Cassie wanted to join me upstairs. I've got some clothes that I don't really need and I wondered if they would be any good for her."

Mum was still on a high about her scarf and the other things. "No, no. You two go upstairs. Supper won't take me long at all. Dad will be back at about eight thirty. See you two in a while." Mum gave me a smile as well. She was obviously surprised and pleased that her two daughters, who were so well-known for squabbling, were getting on. I have to say, so was I.

But I followed Ella up the stairs immediately. I wanted to check out those clothes . . .

* * *

Up in her old bedroom, Ella moved the suitcases off her bed and sat down. "So, how's life going, Cass?" She patted the bed next to her.

I flopped down on the duvet. "OK, I suppose. I've got my GCSEs after Easter which is a bit of a pain. Got my ears pierced today." I pushed my hair back from my face so that she could have a look.

"You what?" Ella's mouth dropped for a second. "How on earth did you get that past Mum? Has she spotted them yet?"

"She knows all about it. She told me to go ahead – after Ruth spoke to her about it, anyway. Because Ruth had her navel pierced today, you see. And I think Mum was so worried that I was going to have something terrible done – you know, by someone at school or something like that, that she let me have my ears pierced." I could tell by Ella's expression that she was impressed.

"Way to go, Cass. Wow! Mum wouldn't let me have mine done until I'd left school. The earrings look good, too. So what else is happening? Any men on the scene yet?" Ella flicked her beautiful hair back with her perfectly manicured hands. Could I ever even hope to look as together as she was?

"Well . . ." I wasn't sure what to say but Ella jumped in before I could think about it.

"So there is! I thought there might be. Who is this guy?

How long have you been going out with him? Come on. Tell your big sister."

"Well . . . I'm not really going out with him. For God's sake, don't tell Mum about him. She'll never leave me alone if she hears!" I had butterflies in my tummy at the very thought.

"What do you mean, you're not really going out with him? Either you are or you aren't." Ella started to plait the hair that hung down by the side of her face. She may have become fantastically glamorous but she hadn't changed completely – she'd always plaited her hair when she was tired.

"Promise me, Ella, that you won't tell Mum and Dad – at least not until after I've been out tomorrow night?"

"Sure – but what's so special about tomorrow night?"

"It's my first date with this boy. He's called Tom." I could feel myself blushing. Why couldn't I even talk about the guy without making a fool of myself?

"Hey – so tell me about him. What's Tom like?" Ella seemed to be genuinely interested.

"Well, he's blond, he's quite tall, and he's at college with Ruth's brother. And he looks gorgeous. But that's all I know really. Except that he's meeting me at a party tomorrow night. It's Tiffany's, a girl at school. I'm going to get there with Ruth and her boyfriend Greg so all Mum needs to know is that I'm going to a party with Ruth, OK?"

"Don't worry, cross my heart," Ella made a graceful gesture of it, "I won't tell a soul. So what are you going to wear?"

I told Ella about Ruth's bootlegs and my crop top. "But you see he saw me wearing the crop top the night I met him."

"What colour are these bootlegs, then?" Ella was up and looking through her wardrobe before I could finish telling her they were blue denim. "Think they'd go with this?" She took a delicious purple satin blouse out and floated it in front of me.

"Wow, it's gorgeous! It must have cost a fortune, Ella!"

"I was given it after a shoot I did for *Vogue*. What do you reckon, then? You can wear it if you want."

"Are you sure, Ella? That would be great. Except . . . except . . ."

"Except what?"

"Except this." I stood up and pulled up my jumper to reveal my transfer.

Ella put down the blouse and came over to take a closer look. "Well, my little sister has grown up! How on earth did you get that one past the old woman, Cass?" I could tell that Ella was impressed.

"Actually, it's not the real thing, it's only a transfer that Ruth did for me this afternoon. It's good though, isn't it?"

"Did you say the crop top was white? So how about wearing it with this over the top of it?" She put the satin blouse back in the wardrobe and pulled out a transparent blue chiffon one that had velvet butterflies and flowers on it. If it was possible, it was even more gorgeous than the other one.

"Could I really wear it?" I stroked the blouse – it was the softest of materials and so fantastic to look at you almost wanted to eat it.

"Sure. And your spider tattoo will just peep tantalisingly through your shirt every time you move. Now, what about shoes?" Ella was looking at my Roos and not very admiringly.

"I was going to wear these – why, what's wrong with them? It took me ages to save up for them. They're the latest gear." I was beginning to feel a strop coming on.

"They're certainly the latest thing – but they don't really suit the outfit. Look, you can wear these if they fit you." Ella looked in her wardrobe and pulled out a pair of ballerina pumps that were almost exactly the same blue as the shirt. They were suede with a patent leather toecap – and they were almost as gorgeous as the shirt. Quite frankly, even if they didn't fit, I was prepared to cut my toes off to cram my feet into them. I knew that no one else at the party was going to have clothes that were half as stylish as these ones Ella was lending me.

"They fit!" I felt like Cinderella. "Do you mind if I wear them? Honestly?"

"Course not or I wouldn't be talking to you about them now, would I? Go and put them in your room – but make sure you hang the shirt properly, won't you?" Ella handed it over to me on a padded hanger.

"Thanks, Ella. I'll go and hang it up now."

Ella followed me into my bedroom with the shoes in her hand. She looked at the piles of magazines and laughed. "Some things never change then, do they? Still reading all your mags, I see."

I could feel the blush coming back again.

"Only kidding, sis! You keep reading them – you can get some really good style ideas from them. Come on – we'd better get downstairs and help Mum with the supper."

Dad came home at almost exactly the time that Mum had said he would. He was obviously as pleased as Mum had been to see Ella. Over supper, Ella told us all about her flat: she shared it with four other models who all earned loads of dosh but never had any time to arrange for any work to be done on the flat. They didn't have a loo of their own and had to share a hole in the ground with every other flat on her floor! Can you believe that? Gross! Majorly gross! I thought my mum was going to die when she heard Ella say that. In fact, I think if she'd realised that Ella was going to have to go to the loo like that, she'd never have let her go to Paris in the first place.

Fortunately, Ella suddenly remembered the present she had for Dad and we were able to concentrate on that instead. It turned out that Ella had bought Dad an Yves Saint Laurent tie – it looked like a fantastic sunrise with all these bright oranges and reds. Dad thought it was great.

When we finished our meal, Ella helped me to stack the dishwasher and we giggled about the fact that Mum and Dad hadn't bought the dishwasher until after Ella had gone to France.

"They obviously couldn't handle all those dishes after I'd gone. I must have been the Marigold Queen!" As she shut the dishwasher door and switched on the programme button, Ella whispered to me quietly, "Don't worry about tommorow night. I promise I won't tell Mum and Dad. You'll have a great time."

"Thanks, Ella." I switched off the kitchen light and we both joined Mum and Dad in the living-room for some coffee that Mum had made with the deliciously aromatic stuff Ella had brought over from France. We spent an hour or so exchanging all our gossip and finding out more about the audition Ella had on Tuesday. Then I remembered my 'Countdown to Love'. I ought to be getting my beauty sleep! I had a big day ahead of me tomorrow! So I said goodnight to everyone (Ella winked at me conspiratorially) and went upstairs to dream about Tom. Maybe it might be fun at the party and just maybe I was going to wow Tom with my looks and dynamic personality.

And maybe I might be able to persuade Ella to help me with my party make-up . . .

CHAPTER NINE

LET'S PARTY!

I woke up the next morning and watched the sun streaming through my curtains. As I lay there for a few minutes dozing, my life was still and calm. Then I had this butterfly sensation in my tummy and it suddenly hit me: MY DATE WITH TOM! Reader, I was out of that bed and heading for the bathroom even quicker than I'd have been moving if the latest copy of *Girl Power* had landed on the doormat.

My first priority was my all-important breakfast. I zoomed down to the kitchen to decide which delicious breakfast cereal to tempt my tastebuds with. Perhaps if I fed my brain properly then I would be able to function like a human being and get my life in the right order. This date with Tom just had to be a success!

I sat down at the table with my Scrunchie Munchies (I'd read an article that said they were fortified with four extra vitamins and extra iron) and a glass of orange juice and found a copy of French *Vogue* which my sister must have left on the table. I thumbed through, looking at the stunning models wearing gorgeous outfits. It was hopeless – how could I ever look like them? As I turned more and more pages, and saw more and more wonderful clothes, my heart sank deeper and deeper. Was I even going to be able to wear the clothes that Ella had lent me and look good?

I heard a door open upstairs and looked at the clock. It was only just after eight and it wasn't at all like anyone else in my family to be up at this time. Now eight might not be that early by some people's standards but it is for my mum and dad. After years of working in the theatre and coming home late after shows, nine is more like the sort of time that they might think of stirring from their slumber. I heard footsteps – light and elegant ones, not clumpy ones like mine – coming down the stairs. Ella walked into the kitchen wearing a red kimono and little velvet Japanese flip-flops on her feet. She looked radiant – and I hated her for it. She didn't even have the faintest smudge of mascara under her eyes.

"Morning!" Ella smiled at me as she flicked the kettle on. She started to rummage through a carrier bag of foodie things that she'd brought with her from Paris and pulled out a square teabag that was attached to a little tag. Ella plopped the teabag into a mug and poured on the hot water. Then she grabbed an apple and a banana from the fruit bowl and sat down with me at the table.

"So," Ella was dunking her teabag in the mug and the water was looking a deeper shade of crimson with every dunk, "are you all set for tonight, then?"

I shut the magazine and put down my spoon. "I've got loads to do: my face-pack, my hair, paint my nails. All that sort of thing." I took a swig of my juice and watched Ella as she munched on her apple. She didn't even seem to do that badly – I always seem to make so much noise when I eat one and I'm forever dropping pips down my front and stuff. "Pooh, Ella! What is that stuff you're about to drink? It stinks."

"Does it? I can't smell anything." She put the mug up to her nose and gave it a sniff. "Perhaps I'm used to it. It's a *tisane*, a herbal tea. They're all the rage in French model circles. They're meant to help give you a clear complexion – my agency put me on to them."

"But it really whiffs – how can you drink it?" I screwed up my nose in disgust.

"Well, I have to admit that it took a bit of getting used to." Ella took a swig as if to demonstrate. "I drank it with a little bit of honey in at first but now I just don't think about it."

"Well, you've certainly got great skin." I finished my last mouthful of cereal (fortified with vitamins and iron or not, it was quite disgusting) and took my bowl and spoon over to the dishwasher. "Now, I've got to go upstairs and prepare myself for tonight. Listen, Ella," I turned to my sister who had started to flick through *Vogue* herself, "promise me you won't tell Mum and Dad about Tom, will you? You know how much she'll go on and on about it."

"I told you," Ella tapped the side of her nose, "Mum's the word." Then she laughed. "Well, perhaps not the most appropriate of phrases but you know what I mean! I won't let you down. It's not that long ago that I went through the same problems, you know."

It was true – which was partly why I knew that I didn't want the parents to know about my date with Tom. I remembered very clearly the grief that they put Ella through when she started to go out with a boy called Zeb. Zeb went to a local boys' school and was, well, a bit, a bit . . . not normal. But then who's normal? What I mean about Zeb, I suppose, is that he wore a lot of jewellery and often dyed chunks of his hair outrageous colours. He was also into some pretty weird music and he'd come round to our house and want to sit and listen to it while he and Ella supposedly did their studying together (this was when Ella was doing her GCSEs). Mum and Dad were convinced that Zeb was into drugs as well as the music. After all, as far as the parents are concerned, anyone who doesn't wear a Marks and Spencer outfit must be a complete degenerate.

"Thanks, Ella." I started to move as if I was going upstairs and then I stopped and turned round. "You know, it's good to see you back." I smiled at my sister, almost not believing that I had heard myself say it.

"It's good to be here but I'm not back," Ella laughed. "I'm here for a week or so – that's all. Once you've left home, you'll know what I mean. I'm not coming back to Mummy and Daddy. Brrr," she pretended to shudder, "nice as they are really, no thanks!"

Once I was back in my bedroom, I picked up my 'Countdown to Love' checklist that I'd written. It said:

1 Tone and cleanse.
2 De-fuzz legs.
3 Face-pack.
4 Make-up.
5 Get dressed.
6 Go.

But when I started on my checklist, it didn't turn out to be quite so straightforward, of course. In fact, it turned out like this:

1 I was about to launch into the face bit when I realised that the de-fuzzing equipment was in the bathroom and by the time I'd finished my face, there was a good chance that my parents would probably be occupying the bathroom (this is the biggest hazard of having parents who don't get up that early – although, of course, it can also be a benefit – after all, they aren't in the bathroom first thing in the morning). I felt very uneasy about changing my plan – after all, the magazine journalists must surely have worked out exactly what they wanted us to do and when for a good reason – don't you think? But I'd made up my mind: I was off to the bathroom to de-fuzz! But how come you never see anyone doing this on the telly?

2 I'd only just covered my legs with shaving foam when Mum tried to barge her way into the bathroom. "Ella, is that you, darling?" Thank goodness Ella had managed to persuade my parents to put a lock on the bathroom door a few years ago (Mum had a problem with not wanting a lock for years as a result of Ella once locking herself in the loo to escape having to listen to a tape-recording of herself singing, aged two and a half. My dad had had to break the door down to get her out).

"No it's me, Cassie. Mum, I'm on the loo!" I shouted. "I'll be out in a minute."

So I ended up shaving my legs really quickly and, of

course, I fouled up badly. Not only did I manage to get blobs of shaving foam on the floor tiles but I also managed to cut myself just by the ankle with the razor. Brilliant, brilliant, brilliant. Great start. Not only did I have to apply half a dozen plasters to my lacerated legs but I ended up having to slop out the bathroom as well.

Then I wrapped my dressing-gown neatly around me (I was sure it made my bum look enormous but at least no one else was looking) and unlocked the bathroom door. I peeped out: the landing was clear! I legged it to my bedroom and managed to close myself in there before Mum was out of Ella's room. Result!

3 Having cleansed and toned, I'd put on the latest Sisters Cool CD while I sank back on my bed, face-pack applied, to read the latest copy of *Celeb* magazine. (*Celeb* was about the only magazine that my parents and I both liked. It was full of interviews with film and television personalities and had loads of photos of them in their fantastic houses.) I thumbed through until I found an interview with the most gorgeous film star of the decade, Pedro Picasso. He was just divine and the article had pictures of him reclining in his marble bath and lounging by his oval-shaped pool. Scrummy. I wondered if Tom looked as gorgeous in his swimming trunks as he did in his jeans. I was just forming a picture of him when there was a knock at the door.

Exasperated, I flung the magazine down on the bed. "Who ish it?" I muttered, trying hard to talk without cracking my face-pack (it was one of those hard ones that has to set).

"It's Ella. Ruth's here with me. Can we come in? We've brought you some coffee and Ruth's got some jeans for you."

"Yeash, shursh," I mumbled through clenched teeth. "Closhe the doorh behind yoush." (It was at this point, dear reader, that I gave up any hope of following my checklist. OK – I'm just not cool in reality!)

"You all right, Cass?" Ruth came in first, clutching her bootlegs. "Have you got toothache?" Then she looked at me and burst out laughing. That really made me feel good, I can tell you. "So that's your problem, a face-pack. Here, Ella, take a look at this!" Ruth was still giggling as Ella came into the room carrying a tray loaded with three mugs of coffee and the biscuit tin. Ella shut the door with her foot and gave a laugh as she put the tray down on the floor. Even I began to see the funny side and it was difficult to stop myself from giggling with them.

"Hey, you really are taking this seriously, aren't you, Cass?" Ella handed me and Ruth our mugs.

Seriously? Wasn't life a pretty serious thing? We only had one chance so we had to get it right, didn't we? As I tried to work out how I could sip my coffee while I had this china-like mask on my face, Ruth answered Ella for me.

"Cassie's got this magazine article about how to get ready for a date. It tells you all the things you've got to do and when. You know, so that everything is perfect."

"Any chance I can take a look at it?" Ella reached over to grab my copy of *Celeb*.

"No, thish ishn't it." I put *Celeb* down and reached over to my bedside magazine rack (if you've got as many magazines as I have, you need one rack near the bed to keep the latest copies of everything near to hand). I found the 'Countdown' and handed it to Ella.

"Here it ish. You look at it while I go to the bathroom and wash thish lot off. Hash Mum gone off to the shtudio yet?"

"Yep, don't worry. Mum and Dad have both gone to work. So you've got until this afternoon to strut your stuff without being found out."

My face-pack had set so hard that it took ages for me to get it all off. I had the stuff up my nose and all over my hair-line. They hadn't said anything about *that* on the tube. Still, I was going to be washing my hair later so I'd be able to get it off then. In the meantime, I blew my nose in an attempt to rid my nostrils of the evidence. The last thing I needed was for Tom to think I had a bogey nesting up there.

Once I'd got everything off, I stood back and gave myself a glance in the mirror. I still had *that* spot! Would nothing shift it? I bunged on some Blitzzit and hoped that it would work miracles by eight o'clock that night. Then I went back into my bedroom to paint my toenails.

By the time my mum and dad came home from work, Ella, Ruth and I had pampered and preened me until even I had to admit that I looked vaguely good. We'd even had a really good time getting me that way, which really surprised me! As I told you earlier, before she'd gone to France, Ella and I didn't get on very well. But now, we seemed to be interested in so many similar things. We both loved clothes and magazines and were both keen to look good. The big difference, though, was that Ella seemed to have life sussed and was more relaxed about things than I was. You could tell from the way that she spoke about stuff that Ella wore things because she liked them rather than because she thought she ought to wear them or because someone had said she should. Let's face it – Ella had confidence. And I didn't.

Anyway, Ella showed Ruth and me loads of tricks she had learned from the professional make-up artists that had done her make-up at fashion shoots and shows (no matter how many more beauty mags I read, I doubt I'd have found out many of Ella's tips). She did my hair and my make-up for me and it looked great – she'd managed to make me look almost as if I didn't have any make-up on

103

but I still looked good. She painted my nails with this brilliant new nail varnish she'd got. It was called Zapping and it was the most brilliant shade of purple. She told me that the next morning, I'd be able to take it off without polish remover – all I had to do was peel it off! She put a transfer on the little fingernail of my left hand as well. Ruth thought everything looked great and she was thrilled when Ella did her nails for her as well. Ruth went for a green colour and it looked brilliant.

When her nails were dry, Ruth zoomed off home to get changed. "I'll be back in about an hour with Greg to collect you. *Ciao, bella!* See you, Ella. And thanks!"

"Pleasure, Ruth," Ella waved at her as she started to disappear down the stairs, "have a great time!"

"See you later, Ruth!" I called. I rubbed my stomach – I had a distinct touch of the butterflies. Oh grief! I thought. What if I throw up all over Tom? I could almost feel my face turning green. Now that would spoil even Ella's make-up!

"What's up?" Ella asked. "Feeling a bit wobbly?"
"Er . . . yeah . . . something like that. My stomach's rumbling with nerves."

"Well, you're bound to be a bit nervous – I remember I was on my first date. What you need is something to eat." Ella rubbed my shoulder reassuringly.

I couldn't imagine that Ella had ever felt nervous. I'd

certainly never picked up on it when she was still living at home.

However the thought of food made me feel sick. And being sick definitely *didn't* have a place in my beauty routine.

"Thanks, Ella, but I don't think I could eat anything."

"Come on – let's make you an omelette or something. If you don't eat anything at all you'll feel worse. Really you will. I remember not eating before a date once and I almost passed out later in the evening. And that was after my stomach had rumbled incredibly noisily throughout the evening! You can imagine how much that impressed my date! Now, let's get off to that kitchen and make the omelette before Mum and Dad are back."

Ella was right. I did need something to eat and the omelette was delicious. While I ate (Ella was going to wait to eat with Mum and Dad) Ella told me about some of the disastrous dates she'd been on. Some of the stories were hysterical: one bloke had taken her for a boating trip and had then lost the oars in the middle of the river – they had to wait to be rescued by another boat; then there was another guy who had taken her out for a slap-up meal and had then discovered that he hadn't got his wallet with him so Ella had to pay for all of it! I began to think that, almost whatever happened, my evening couldn't possibly be that bad.

I'd almost finished eating when the phone rang. As Ella chatted to a friend I started to think a bit more about what possible disasters I would have to live through tonight. Or perhaps I wouldn't? Maybe it would be wonderfully romantic! Maybe Tom would bring me a gorgeous red rose! Or would he give me a gentle kiss that made my neck tingle? Would I see stars? Make dynamic conversation? And have witty and intelligent answers to all his soul-searching questions?

I looked at my watch and realised I needed to get a move on. I slipped past Ella up to my room.

Mum and Dad came home while I was still upstairs changing and I could hear them chatting to Ella about their day. Once I got my clothes on and had applied the lip-gloss that Ella had left out for me, I sneaked into my parents' room to take a good look at myself. Hmmm. Not bad. I turned round to look at my back view. Could be better (a bit smaller perhaps) but not too bad. I had a final, close-up look at my face. Hmmm. I still had that spot but Ella had covered it up with something and it wasn't quite so obvious as before.

I looked at my watch and almost exactly at the same time, I heard the doorbell. It must be Ruth and Greg. Mum answered the door and was chatting away to her beloved Ruth. I'd mentioned the party to Mum and Dad the night before when we were having supper with Ella. They weren't too hysterical about it (you know, not too many questions about how many drug pushers were going to be there and could they have the inside leg measurement of Tiffany's father) really, but I could still hear Mum quizzing Ruth – she was obviously just checking that Ruth came up with the same answers about how we were getting there and when we would be home.

Back in my room, I grabbed my coat and gave my hair a final brush. Then I steamed down the stairs. "Hi, Mum! Bye, Mum!" I went head-first for the door. I was hoping that I could make a quick getaway.

"Cassie! Wait! Let's see what you look like!" Mum grabbed my arm, stopping my exit.

Greg gave an approving whistle which managed to make me blush. "Wow, Cass! You look – great!"

"You look really good, Cass." Ruth added.

"Er, thanks, er . . ." I just couldn't handle it. I'd thought it was bad enough when people told you you looked awful but when someone tells you you look good, what are you meant to say?

"Yes, Cassie, you look very nice, dear." Mum sounded surprised. Thanks for all your maternal support, Mother dear! "But what's that black thing on your stomach?"

Oh boy, she'd spotted my spider. Now how was I going to get out of the house?

"Sorry to be in a rush, Mrs Lang . . ." Ruth turned on

her usual charm. But it didn't work. Mum was still staring at the spider.

So then Ella moved in on her. "Hey, Mum!" she called from the living-room. "You promised you'd show me your latest photos from the studio. Where are they?"

"Just a minute, Ella." Mum's loyalties were clearly being stretched as she looked back into the living-room at Ella and then back at me. Thankfully, Ella's attentions won.

"Well, bye then. Have a great time. I'll talk to you when you get back, Cassie." Mum was obviously determined to keep in control of me. I certainly wouldn't believe she was going to let the transfer go without further comment.

"Bye, Mum. Bye, Ella, Dad!" I called over my shoulder and down the hall to the living-room as I left.

"Bye, Mrs Lang!" Ruth trooped down the path with me, closely followed by Greg. I could see Sam waiting for us at the corner – he had obviously been wisely warned off coming to see my mum by Ruth.

Further up the road, I could see a bus already coming. Sam had spotted it and was calling us to hurry up. As we got closer, we could see that there wasn't just one bus but three.

We hopped on the first bus, paid our fares and sat down on the long seat at the back. We were all grinning and laughing – clearly we were all in the party mood. When she got her breath back, Ruth spoke first: "Typical," she said, "buses are just like boys. One minute there isn't a man in sight and the next three come along at the same time!"

We all laughed and then I sat back and thought about it in silence for a moment. Forget three boys – I just hoped I could cope with one . . .

CHAPTER TEN

ALL THE BEST THINGS IN LIFE TAKE A BIT OF GETTING USED TO

Tiffany's mum and dad are really loaded with cash. They live in this great big house even though Tiffany hasn't got any brothers and sisters. The three of them must rattle around inside it. Tiffany's OK but she can be a bit of a show-off at times – she's lucky, you see, because she gets this enormous allowance from her parents every month so she can buy almost anything she wants to when she wants to. Lucky her. But, actually, I sometimes wonder if it's really that lucky. You see,

Tiffany is quite popular at school, although Ruth and I aren't really in her crowd. But most of the girls who hang out with Tiffany are a bit shallow, if you know what I mean. They don't bother much with their schoolwork and Ruth and I often get the impression that one of the attractions of being Tiffany's mate is the fact that she's got dosh and takes all of her crowd out on a hooley every now and then. When Tiffany falls out with someone, she falls out big-time: her victim gets sent to Coventry by all of Tiffany's clique for ages and they really have to crawl to get back in. Perhaps it's because I'm lucky enough to have a mate like Ruth that I can't be bothered to do all the sucking up to Tiffany that she requires.

The four of us got off the bus and walked up the road towards Tiffany's house. Just as we were coming up to the front drive, this small, dark car came down the road towards us. It had darkened windows and lots of shiny chrome bits – a real pose-mobile. As the car pulled in to park, the horn was sounded: da da dada dada dada da da da da – it was the Dixieland theme.

"What a nerd!" Sam said as we turned into the drive.

"You bet – plonker," said Greg and we all giggled.

Before we got to the front door, though, the driver leaped out and called, "Cassie! Cassie! How's my gorgeous girl?"

I turned round, wondering who on earth it was.

"Cassie!" The car's owner grabbed me round the waist and tilted me over sideways like some kind of Latin American ballroom dancer. From my semi-upside-down position, I could see Sam, Greg and Ruth standing in silence. I'm sure that Sam's jaw was actually open in disbelief.

I struggled to get myself on to my feet again, and when I did, I was given a kiss on the cheek that literally made a smacking sound. I pushed my assailant away from me and said, "Excuse me." And that was when I saw his face.

It was Tom . . .

I could feel the butterflies fluttering around in my stomach and I started to cough. Oh boy – was I going to puke? Wasn't this the moment I was meant to be seeing stars in my eyes? Wasn't I meant to feel lighter than air? Instead, I could feel my heart sinking a bit. None of the magazines had mentioned how to cope with a situation like this!

Before I knew what was happening, Tom was whisking me up to the front door. I turned and looked at Ruth, who was looking on with a surprised expression on her face. Was this really the same boy that we saw at the sports centre last weekend? As Tiffany opened the door, I tried to calm myself down.

"Hi, Tom!" Tiffany gushed and went to put her arm around him. Then she caught sight of me (and the arm that Tom had firmly around my shoulders) and pulled her arm back.

"C-Cassie. Hello. I didn't realise that you were coming." She gave me a frosty smile. I could see her eyeing my Prada bag. Clearly she knew what it was but she probably assumed it was a fake. The frosty smile seemed more than frosty. It was frozen.

Oh great, I thought. Not only was I at Tiffany's party in the presence of the owner of a pose-mobile but he hadn't even told the host of the party that he was bringing me. (OK, OK – so I told Tom that I was going to Tiffany's party, but that was, well – OK, that was a lie! I'd fibbed, which was probably why Tom hadn't told Tiffany I was coming with him.)

"Hi, Tiffany – er, happy birthday." I gave her the card and the bubble bath that I'd brought for her present but she didn't look overly enthusiastic about it. She probably drowned in expensive bubbles every night. Or bathed in asses' milk like Elizabeth Taylor did when she was playing Cleopatra in that old movie.

Ruth stepped into the hall behind me and used her usual charm and diplomacy to diffuse the situation. "Tiffany, happy birthday. Great dress – was it a present?" The dress had obviously cost a small fortune and Ruth had done exactly what Tiffany had wanted by commenting on it.

"Yes, actually my parents bought it for me in the States at Christmas. We went over there for the skiing, you know – Aspen. Sam, Greg – thanks for coming. You too, Ruth."

Some more people were coming up the drive behind us so Tiffany ushered us in to the party. "It's upstairs, you guys, in my annex. Go straight up to the top – head for the music."

"Annex? What annex?" Greg said to Ruth as they headed up the stairs in front of Tom, Sam and me.

"Oh, haven't you heard?" Tom said. "The top of the house is the granny annex, only Tiffany doesn't have a granny that needs it. So her mum and dad have let her move in there as part of her sixteenth birthday present." Tom obviously knew Tiffany quite well I was beginning to realise.

"You mean she's already got her own flat?" Sam whistled in disbelief and approval at the same time.

"Wow!" I exclaimed and then I realised that Tom and the others were looking at me. I could feel myself blushing. What a stupid, childish thing to say! For a first date, this was not going well – and it certainly wasn't what I'd been expecting. Shouldn't I be feeling wildly glamorous and exciting?

We got to Tiffany's part of the house and walked into a large room which looked like something out of an interior designers' magazine. It was gorgeous – there were ethnic rugs hanging on the walls and two gorgeous sofas which were pushed back against the wall. Some girls from school (none of the boys from college, of course) were already dancing in the middle of the room to the latest

Bad Boyz CD and there was a table with a buffet laid out and cans of Coke and beer. The lighting was low. Tom took my hand and led me across the room. "Cassie, my love," he kissed my hand and I could feel myself tingling with pleasure, "what would you like to drink?"

"Er," I pulled my hand away before I fainted, "a Coke, please."

"Sure?" Tom leaned closer to me. "Sure you don't want a drop of the hard stuff?"

"No, thanks. A Coke would be fine." I didn't want to be legless on my first date with Tom. And anyway, how could I admit that I didn't even like the taste of beer?

As Tom grabbed the drinks and led me over to the corner where there were some floor cushions I looked over to Ruth, who was already chatting to some of Greg and Sam's friends from college. She never seemed to have a problem finding the right thing to say to the right person. Ruth caught my eye and waved. Then she started to laugh at a joke someone had obviously just told. I made a conscious decision to try to behave like that and frantically started to wrack my brains to think of some jokes.

Tom sat himself down on a cushion and patted the one next to him, indicating that he wanted me to sit down with him. I knelt down and managed to pour some of my Coke over the cushion.

"Oops!" Tom laughed. "Don't tell Tiff." (Did he know

her that well? I wouldn't dare to call her that!) "Quick! Let's turn the cushion over and then she'll never know."

I finally sat down and realised how close I was to Tom. I could almost feel his breath on my cheek. So I sat back and crossed my legs in a kind of ballet 'Frog' position. It made me feel a bit like one of my mum's pupils in her toddler class but at least it gave me some distance from Tom and made me feel more in control of the situation.

"So, Cassie. You look lovely tonight." Tom swigged from his can of beer. "Really gorgeous. I love your nails – is the diamond real?" Tom pointed to the fake gems that Ella had put on for me.

"Course not." I put my can of Coke down. "My sister did it for me. She's a model and she's over from France at the moment."

"A model? Really?" Clearly Tom was impressed and I spent the next half-hour or so telling Tom all about Ella and her life. It was much easier talking about her than thinking of things to say about myself. I'd just about got to the bit about Ella being over to try out for the cosmetic company when Sam came over with a girl he was at college with.

"Hey, you guys. Is this a private party or can any of us join in?" Sam and the girl sank down on the floor. They'd been dancing and were clearly very hot and in need of a rest and the cans of Coke that they were swigging from. "Cassie, meet Toni. Toni, Cassie." We smiled and said hello to each other. "And this, as you know, is Tom."

"Hi, Toni," Tom raised his hand as if to wave. "How'ya doing?"

"Fine, thanks. It's a good party, isn't it? Isn't this house just great?" Toni looked at me and smiled again. "You been here before, Cassie?"

"No, no I haven't. I'm at school with Tiffany though," (well done, Cassie, the way to impress by proving how juvenile you are), "but we're not really good friends." (That must have really sounded great: a kind of "I hate her, actually, but I still came to her party".)

Toni laughed a little, though not unkindly. Then she, Sam and Tom started to chat about some of their mates from college – they were obviously people they knew well and I couldn't think of a thing to say. I remembered one of the magazine articles from *Girl Power* that gave twenty tips for how to handle a situation like this. The first tip was to listen carefully to the chat and agree with things that other people were saying. So I sat there nodding my head and saying "yes" and "absolutely" as often as I could. Every now and then Toni gave me a strange sort of look. Sam gave me the odd smile almost as if he was encouraging me to join in. Tom didn't seem to take much notice because he was so busy gassing away. After a while I gave up nodding – apart from anything else, it was making my neck ache.

I let my eyes gaze around the room. By now there were quite a few people at the party. I could see Tiffany flirting like crazy with a bloke who looked like he was in his twenties. He was quite good-looking but nothing that special. I wondered if he was the guy called Henry that I'd heard Tiffany going on about at lunch the other day. She kept on telling everyone how she'd met him at her cousin Will's – apparently he was at university with him. Whatever, however much attention Tiffany gave him, he didn't seem to be that bothered. In fact, if anything, he looked a bit bored. To my horror, I suddenly realised that he was staring at me staring at him! I was shaken out of my reverie and could feel myself blushing. Henry, or whoever he actually was, started to smile at me and winked. I turned away in horror and started to look around the rest of Tiffany's flat.

It looked as if Tiffany had her own bedroom and bathroom, as well as a very small kitchen up in her annex. Can you imagine it? A place to call your own? Nice one. Just like one of those rich kids in a movie. There was a couple snogging in the doorway of the bedroom. I thought I recognised the girl from school but to be honest I couldn't be certain – anyway, I was too fascinated by what they were actually doing. Where exactly did she put her tongue? And supposing he'd just eaten a piece of pizza? Yuck! They never mentioned that in the magazine article about snogging.

I was beginning to feel a bit faint, so I let my eyes wander further around the room. I waved at some of my other friends from school and I spotted Ruth having another animated conversation with someone. I couldn't hear what it was about above the noise of the music but I wished that I was as involved in the conversation near me as she was with hers. I felt a faint tap on my shoulder.

"Would you, Cassie?"

I turned round to the direction of the tap. It was Tom doing the tapping.

"Hi – are you still with us?" Tom gave me one of his delicious smiles and I began to feel happy again. This must surely be more like it was meant to be.

"Sorry," I laughed in what I hoped was a coquettish manner, "I didn't catch that – I was just waving to some-one I know over there." I hoped I sounded a bit more worldly-wise.

"Sure," Tom nodded his head knowingly. "I was just wondering if you would like to have a dance and then something to eat. Or would you prefer to do it the other way round?"

"Oh, let's dance." This was it – the moment I had been waiting for. I'd watched an old movie called *Saturday Night Fever* with my mum not long ago and I'd been dying to dance with a really good boy. I'd been imagining dancing with Tom – him smooching up close to me in his white suit, dancing cheek to cheek with me and running his fingers through mine. Phew – it was hot stuff.

The music was perfect. I may not be Tiffany's best mate but she has great taste in music. She's not just into the latest chart-toppers, but she has some quite unusual stuff – all great dancing music. I hit the dance floor in a state of excitement, but, dear reader, I'm afraid it wasn't quite what I had expected . . .

Tom may have been a great basketball player but he just wasn't such a good dancer. It was bad enough when he was treading on my toes and generally ignoring the rhythm of the songs. But then he grabbed my hands and tried to swirl me round the room! I didn't feel cool, I felt self-concious – and red. This wasn't how it was done in the films! But gradually I realised that everyone wasn't staring at us. And anyway, it wasn't me that would look bad, it would be Tom. And really, Tom was probably as good a dancer as anyone else at the party. So, bearing in mind that he was rather hunky and good-looking, what did it matter? Maybe I might even look a little bit cool. It wasn't fireworks, but it was fun.

Tom and I danced for at least half an hour before we stopped. We were both feeling hot so when Tom suggested we grab something to eat and go to sit over by the kitchen window, which someone had opened, I agreed. We loaded up our plates at the buffet spread, grabbed something to drink and wandered out of the crowded room. Ruth was standing near the doorway and mouthed "OK?" at me as I went by. I nodded my head.

The kitchen was empty except for the plates of people's leftovers and other food stuff which hadn't been laid out yet. There was a kind of window seat for us to sit on and I put my plate down and got myself organised before I sat down to eat. Tom gave me another of his delicious smiles and leaned over to give me a slow kiss on the cheek.

"Cassie, you are a terrific dancer and you look great tonight." It was just like that moment in the movie – you know, *Let's Party*.

"Er . . . thanks," I said, looking down at my plate. Dancing with Tom in a crowded room was one thing. But to sit alone with him and receive compliments was another. So I shoved a forkful of coleslaw in my mouth and munched while I thought of the next thing to say.

Tom put his fork down and leaned over towards me again. "I think this is yours – oops." He picked up a piece of coleslaw that I'd obviously dropped from my last forkful straight on to Ella's blouse. Uncool. (That hadn't happened in the movie.) Possibly a stain as well – Ella might kill me when I got home.

"Hey, what's that?" Tom was stroking my waist – he'd spotted my spider transfer! "Hey, wow – you've got a tattoo! Did it hurt?"

I cannot deny how good it felt to have really impressed Tom! But I was then stupid enough to admit that it was only a transfer and not the real thing. Even so, he still seemed impressed – and he was still stroking my waist and I wasn't at all certain how to handle it. I swallowed hard and put my fork down before removing his hand and placing it back on his leg. Tom smiled at me and I got the distinct impression that he knew I was feeling slightly out of control of the situation. I tried to think of something to say and hoped that what I was about to say wasn't going to sound too boring.

"So, what are you studying at college, Tom?"

"History, English and French. I'm doing my A levels – I couldn't stand the thought of staying on at my old school to do them. Anyway, there's so much more opportunity to do sports at college than there was at the boys' school. And I want to go off to university afterwards – perhaps to study sports sciences, I'm not sure. But how about you – what are you studying?"

I prattled on about how hard it had been to decide between Biology and Human Biology. At one point I could have sworn that he was looking over at a girl near the kitchen doorway. But, anyway, I carried on telling Tom all about my GCSE subjects.

"But I haven't really decided what I want to do for my A levels yet." I stopped talking for a bit – I was sure Tom had winked at her. He turned back to me but as I was talking I could see that his eyes were looking a bit glazed. I remembered one of my magazine articles: look animated as you speak. So I waved my arms around excitedly as I carried on. "You see, until recently I thought I was going to go off to a dancing college but then I realised that it wasn't what I really wanted to do. So my future is a bit up in the air. I'd quite like to do Classical Civilisation as one of my subjects but my mum reckons I'd be better off doing History – which is a bit rich coming from her and bearing in mind she never got much in the way of qualifications herself."

Tom's eyes were wandering over towards the other food that was sitting on the work surface.

"Tom? Is something wrong?" I sort of waved my hands animatedly in front of his eyes.

"What? Oh no – I know what you mean – parents always know best." So he was listening to me. I couldn't imagine Tom being bullied into anything by his parents. "But you're not going to stay at school after your GCSEs, are you? You are going to come to college? You'd love it there! You'd be great there! And I could show you off to all of my mates!"

I couldn't believe what he'd just said! This was our first date and Tom was already talking about the future. Perhaps I wasn't doing so badly after all.

Tiffany came into the kitchen to get the rest of the food and seemed a bit put out to find us there. "Oh – it's you two." She gave me (being one of the two) a frosty glare. "I just came in to get the rest of the food and my cake out of the fridge. It's an ice-cream one, you know – made especially for me by a department store in central London."

By now, Tom and I had finished our food so I gathered up our plates quickly and put them with the other dirty ones on the side.

"Here, Tiffany, let's help you. What do you want us to take in for you? How can we help?" I gave Tiffany one of my most gushing smiles (something very useful I'd learned to do at the many dancing competitions I'd been entered into during my childhood) and she seemed to lighten up a bit.

"You could take in the plates please, Cassie." Tiffany handed them to me. Tom just stood there. He was sideways on to us, staring at one of the windowpanes. I wasn't unconvinced that he wasn't looking at his reflection in the glass. Surely he couldn't be?

"Here, Tom," I elbowed him in the ribs and he seemed to jump out of his reverie, "why don't you take those two plates of food in for Tiffany?"

"Oh." He looked a bit surprised to be asked to do something. "OK, I will." Was this guy for real? Could he really have been looking at his reflection? Was Tom as vain as that? Surely my date wasn't supposed to do that? I was beginning to wonder if Tom was all I'd set him up to be.

Tiffany led the way back into the living-room and we followed. She had the plate with her cake on it and was clearly really chuffed with it. Back in the kitchen she'd lit the candle on it. It was a sort of fizzy thing a bit like a fire-work and everyone stopped dancing, eating and talking and looked at it. Someone called out, "Happy birthday, Tiffany!" and we all started to sing to her. Then Tom rushed over to Tiffany and gave her a great big kiss on the cheek. I wish I could say that I felt cool about it. But I didn't.

Tiffany cut her cake and we all sat down to scoff it. It was delicious – just like that really scrummy ice-cream that has the steamy ads in the magazines. Ruth and Greg came over to join us. So did Sam and Toni. Sam seemed to have been with Toni for most of the evening and I wondered if she was his new girlfriend. Certainly he'd never mentioned having a girlfriend before – but then I suppose I'd never spoken to him that much. The six of us chatted for a while and then the mood of the music changed. Suddenly it wasn't fast dancing music but a slow record. Ruth and Greg got up to dance. So did Sam and Toni. That left me and Tom on our own. The conver-sation dried up. I was desperate for Tom to ask me to dance again. But I was also desperately worried – if he did ask me, what would I do with my hands? My head? Where would I look?

"Come on, Cassie. Let's dance." Tom pulled me gently up to the dance floor and put his arms round me.

Oh my goodness. I could feel myself getting hot – and sweaty. I was certain that I must have great wet marks under my arms. Perhaps I even smelt of BO! They never mentioned any of this in the magazines! I felt like a wooden doll (and I knew what one was meant to feel like because I'd once danced a wooden doll dance in a dancing competition). Tom didn't seem to notice though – he was too busy getting on with the dance on his own despite the fact that he'd got his arms round me. No, slow dancing was certainly not meant to be like this. I knew because I'd read all about it. And seen it in plenty of films.

I was relieved when the song was over and Ruth and Greg came over to us. "We've got to get going, Cass." Ruth gave me a strange sort of look. She was obviously wondering if I wanted to go home with them or stay with Tom. In reality, I wanted to do both – only I didn't think I could handle being in the car with Tom on my own.

"Yes – so have I. I'd better be getting back."

"Oh no, Cassie," Tom held my arm, "don't leave me now." He sounded like a bad actor in an afternoon soap.

"Sorry, Tom. I've had a really great evening. Thanks for

everything. Thanks for bringing me here tonight!" I smiled even though I knew he hadn't actually brought me there – and surprise, surprise, I started to blush again.

"Let me give you a lift home." Tom was still holding my arm.

I was certain that I couldn't handle being in the car on my own with him. Supposing he tried to kiss me?

"Um, er . . . that would be great, Tom! We'd love a lift! Ruth lives round the corner from me, you see!" I tried to sound like I was bubbly, not panicky. I'm not sure that Tom was impressed.

Anyway, we said our thanks and our goodbyes to Tiffany. Then we set off for the journey home in Tom's car. As he put the key in the car door, I was certain I saw him looking at his reflection in the car window . . .

It didn't take long to get home and I sat in the back with Ruth. Greg made us all laugh by telling us some of the terrible jokes he'd got off the Internet and the atmosphere was really quite relaxed by the time we pulled up outside my house.

"Cassie my darling, I've got you home." Tom opened his door and pulled the seat forward so that I could get out. He took my hand and kissed it as he helped me out.

"Cassie, Cassie." He held both of my hands with his. I hoped my mum wasn't watching from behind the living-room curtains.

"Thanks, Tom. For a great evening." I pulled my hands away from his – they were a bit clammy for my liking. Why wasn't I feeling up in the heavens? Somehow he made me feel uncomfortable and I was sure it wasn't meant to feel this way. Shouldn't I be feeling like I couldn't bear to say goodnight? You know, "Parting is such sweet sorrow," and all that?

"Thank you, Cassie," Tom kissed me on the forehead before he climbed back in the car. "I'll give you a call tomorrow!"

I was speechless. Did this mean that Tom wanted to see me again?

"Night, Cass!" Greg and Ruth called to me.

"Er, night, you guys!" I answered and then set off up the path to the front door as Tom's car pulled away.

As soon as I was inside, Mum was standing at the living-room door. "I thought you went to the party with Ruth and Greg," she said with a suspicious look in her eyes. "I didn't think Greg drove. Whose car was that?"

Mothers . . .

CHAPTER ELEVEN

A LIFE
MORE
ORDINARY

I went into the living-room, hoping that there might be safety from my mum if I wasn't on my own. Thank goodness Ella was still up and Dad was in the room.

"Hi!" Ella gave me an encouraging smile. She was sitting on the floor going through all our old photo albums. They'd obviously been having an evening of reminiscence. Gosh, what a shame I'd missed it . . .

"Did you have a good evening, sweetie?" Dad put his mug of coffee down and looked at me. He was smiling as well. I think he had an idea of what my mum was about to put me through.

"Yes thanks, Dad. It was great. There were lots of girls from school there and some of Greg's mates from college."

Mum sat down next to Dad on the sofa and then she started. "So, was it one of Greg's friends that brought you home? I certainly haven't seen Greg driving before." She was sitting bolt upright.

"Yes it was. He dropped me off before he dropped Ruth and Greg off round the corner. Have you had a good evening?" I was trying to put Mum off the scent.

Ella stood up and said, "I was just going to make myself another cup of coffee, Cass. Do you want one?"

I quite fancied one but I wasn't sure if I wanted to sit down here with Mum for any longer than I needed to. On the other hand, why put off the inevitable nosiness until tomorrow morning? So I relented.

"Yes, thanks. Do you want some help?" I scurried out of the room and followed Ella to the kitchen. I called over my shoulder, "Mum, Dad, do you want any more?" They shook their heads before Mum started to whisper to Dad. She was obviously telling him about the car.

Ella partly shut the kitchen door behind me and switched on the kettle. I busied myself with getting the mugs ready for our coffee.

"So," Ella whispered. "How did it go? Is he as nice as you'd hoped?"

"Er, yes. I think so. To be honest, I'm not sure. His car's a bit naff. You know, all black and chrome with a really nerd-like horn that plays a tune. Not really what I expected.

Still, he says he's going to ring me tomorrow. We'll see if he does."

"Do you want him to?" Ella poured the water into the mugs and stirred.

"Yes." I took the mugs and opened the door with my foot.

Back in the living-room, Mum and Dad were listening to a CD.

"So, what did you say the boy driving the car was called?" I knew Mum wouldn't be able to resist it.

"I didn't, Mum. But his name is Tom. He's a student at college with Greg and he's studying English, History and French. He's hoping to go to university and no, I don't know where he lives. OK? Satisfied now? Oh yes, and he plays basketball for his college team." I took a sip of my coffee and managed to burn my lip. I couldn't even drink a cup of coffee without burning myself! You never saw any of the soap stars burning themselves. Nor any movie stars. Except the fat guys in the comedies.

"Now there's no need to talk to your mother like that, Cassie. She was only asking," Dad said tetchily.

"OK, I'm sorry. But why do you have to give me an interrogation? All I've done is go to a party – that's what teenagers do, you know. Go to parties with other teenagers." I looked deep into my coffee mug, rather wishing I could drown in it. Why did I have to react? If I just let it go, then Mum probably wouldn't make that much of it.

"I was only asking who you were with." Mum looked indignant. "And who you came home with."

"Well I told you. Tom. OK? Look, I'm off to have a bath and go to bed. Night."

Ella was tidying up the photograph albums. "Night, Cass," she winked at me (I seemed to do a lot of communicating with people via winks these days).

I zoomed upstairs and started to run the bath. There was some delicious-looking bubble bath on the side which I poured in. It must have been Ella's. It smelled delicious too. I left the bath running while I went to my room and undressed. I carefully hung the clothes up and looked at them. I reckoned I had looked good in them that night, even if I had spilled coleslaw on Ella's blouse.

And I reckoned that Tom thought so to.

I wrapped my dressing-gown round me and shoved on my slippers – a totally un-cool pair of dinosaur's feet that my gran had given me for Christmas. I made a mental note that I'd better do something about changing them. Then I went and had my bath.

And it was only when I washed off the spider that I realised Mum had forgotten all about it. Phew.

Back in my room, I read a copy of *Clothes Rack* magazine. I could hear the noises of everyone else in the house going to bed. Mum and Dad did their bits and pieces in the bathroom and then I heard the landing light being clicked off. About ten minutes later there was the faintest knock on my door but before I could answer it, Ella poked her head round the door and whispered, "Can I come in?"

"Sure." I put the magazine down and leaned up on one elbow. Ella quietly shut the door and came to sit down on my bed. She was wearing her gorgeous kimono and velvet flip-flops again. Perhaps they were what I should get instead of my dino feet?

"So, tell me all about it, then. What was the party like?"

Ella tucked her knees under her chin and sat looking at me while I told her everything in a whispery voice. I told her about Tiffany's annex (I think even Ella was impressed), the dancing (definitely impressed) and what Tom had talked about.

"I think I do want him to call but I'm not entirely certain he's as great as I thought he was," I whispered honestly when I'd finished telling her about everything else.

"Well, if he rings and asks you out again, then you'll have a chance to find out more about him. And if he doesn't, then you won't lose any sleep over him either."

Ella made it all sound so easy – but it just wasn't. I desperately wanted Tom to call me again tomorrow (even if it did mean that Mum and Dad would know because they were bound to be in all day). It would be a disaster if he didn't – Tiffany and all the other girls at school were bound to ask me more about him when we went back after the holidays. What would I say to them if I didn't hear any more from Tom?

"Well goodnight, sis." Ella rubbed the hair on the top of my head which I have to admit I found extremely irritating. Even so, I was grateful to her for letting me borrow her clothes and for doing my make-up and stuff.

"Thanks, Ella – for your help. And for keeping Mum more under control."

"No problem. Night." And Ella was silently slipping her way back to bed.

I turned off the light and lay back on my pillow. Perhaps, just like in the fairy tales, I could fall asleep and be woken up by a handsome prince. Reader, I dreamed on . . .

I didn't get up that early the next morning but when I did, my conscience made me do some revision for my exams. I was beginning to realise that I no longer had the security blanket of thinking I'll try harder next time. This time round was going to be *the* time so I had to get on with it.

I studied in my room while Mum and Dad went with Ella to see my gran who lived about half an hour away. I'd been working for about an hour when I heard the phone ring and I went to answer the phone in the hall so that I could grab some biscuits (not good for the zits, I know, but good for making you feel better when you are revising Binary Maths) at the same time. I was just about to lift the receiver when I panicked. Supposing it was Tom? What would I say to him? I stood there with my hand on the receiver and did nothing. Susie May (she's that really stunning actress who is always appearing in *Celeb* magazine) never did this in any of the movies when she was waiting for her man to call. She just took the call, looked fantastic and lived happily ever after at the end of the movie.

The phone carried on ringing while I carried on panicking. What to do? In my panic, I suddenly realised that the phone had rung so many times now it was probably going to stop ringing because whoever was calling was going to hang up. I grabbed the receiver.

"Hello?" Did I sound as mad as I felt I did?

"Hey, Cassie!"

"Ruth! Thank goodness it's only you!" I cannot tell you how relieved (and how disappointed) I was.

"Thanks a bunch, BF. So, did you have fun last night? You seemed to be getting along OK."

"I think so but I haven't heard anything from Tom yet. Do you think he'll call?"

"Well, it just so happens that I've just had a call from Greg who's just had a call from Tom . . ."

I interrupted before she had a chance to finish. "What did he phone *him* about?"

". . . saying that he thinks you are quite something and that he wonders if you'd want to come on a foursome date tonight. He's fixed up with Greg for us to go to Pizza-the-Action at seven. So, are you on?"

I was – but at the same time I wondered why Tom was asking Greg and Ruth before he was asking me. Seemed like a bit of a cheek to me. Ruth spoke again before I said anything. "So, are you? Are you still there, Cassie?"

"Yes, of course. Yes, yes I'm still here. But is Tom going to phone me to ask me if I want to go out with him? Or has he just assumed that I'll be coming?" I was a bit miffed, to be honest.

"I think he's going to ring you – at least, I hope he is. You're right, he should be asking you. But I think that's the kind of boy that Tom is." Ruth sounded a bit uncomfortable as she said it.

"What do you mean, 'The kind of boy that Tom is'?" What was Ruth getting at?

"Well . . . he's . . . sort of . . ." It was obvious that Ruth was trying not to be rude. ". . . Well . . . bossy – conceited, I suppose. He always expects *you* to meet *him*." Now she'd said it.

"What do you mean, conceited?" I didn't care how uncomfortable Ruth was, I wanted to find out what she meant.

"I don't know, Cassie! He's your boyfriend, not mine. Go out with him tonight and see what you think! Look, I've got to go – I'm sorting out my History coursework folder. Listen, give me a call if Tom doesn't phone you. Otherwise I'll see you later."

"Yeah, bye." I put the phone down and headed straight for the biscuit tin. Before I'd even realised it, I'd eaten two biscuits. What did Ruth mean, he was conceited? Bossy? Did she mean that he was rude? Or did she actually mean that he wanted me to come running after him? If he did, I wasn't sure that he was the sort of boy I wanted. On the other hand, it was better to have a boyfriend than no boy at all, wasn't it? And beggars couldn't be choosers, could they? Oh – I gave up! None of this rubbish happened to Cinderella – she just got to go to the ball in a great outfit, with a great guy who then topped it all and married her!

I had started to nibble on my third biscuit when the phone rang again. This time I answered it straight away – and I had a mouthful of biscuit.

"Hello?" I said, spraying crumbs around the hall.

"Is Cassie there please?" It *was* Tom.

"Hi, Tom! Yes, this is Cassie!" Even I realised that I sounded too keen.

"Cassie, hi there. How are you?" He didn't actually wait for me to answer. "Listen, I was wondering if you'd like to come out with me tonight? I've been talking to Greg and we thought it might be an idea for you and Ruth to join us for a pizza? You know, the new pizza place in the

High Street? OK? See you there at seven, then. Bye."

"Yes, bye," I replied but before I had a chance to finish, Tom had already put the phone down. Oh well, I
thought, it must be my problem. At least Mum and Dad
hadn't been around to listen in on the phonecall.

I put the receiver down and picked it back up straight
away and dialled Ruth's number. Sam answered.

"Cassie, how are you?" He actually waited for me to
answer.

"OK, thanks. Did you enjoy the party last night? Toni
seems really nice." Nice was such an uncool, juvenile
word – but my brain wasn't thinking quickly enough for
me to find another word.

"Yes, she is. It was a shame though that her boyfriend
couldn't go with her, wasn't it?" So Toni wasn't Sam's girlfriend after all, then.

"Sam, is Ruth still around? If she is, can I speak to her?"

"Sure thing – just a second." Sam went off to get her
and shortly afterwards, Ruth picked up the phone.

"Cass – what can I do for you?"

"Tom rang. Just now. He's invited me to join you
tonight."

"So he's picking you up in his car, then? Are we included
in this journey or do Greg and I make our own way
there?"

"Actually," I felt a bit stupid – and embarrassed – as I

said it, "he's meeting me there. Can I go with you and Greg?" Now I really did feel stupid – as if I was asking them both to hold my hands.

"What, again? Oh well, of course you can come with us, Cass. Why don't you come round at quarter to seven? It'll only take us a short while to get to the High Street."

"OK, see you then. Bye."

I spent the rest of the morning revising. Ella came back from Gran's with Mum and Dad and we all had lunch. Afterwards, when we were loading up the dishwasher, Ella asked if Tom had called. I told her all about it.

"But I'm only going to tell Mum and Dad that I'm going with a bunch of girls from school to the pizza place. You won't let on, will you, Ella?"

"No, course not. Listen, help yourself to another top from my wardrobe – there's a red skinny-rib jumper that would really suit you. You're welcome to borrow it. And you can use the make-up again too."

"Thanks, Ella – it's really kind of you." It was. And I couldn't believe how lucky I was that Ella had come back (and been so nice) at just the right time for me.

When we'd finished sorting out the kitchen, I went back upstairs, telling Mum and Dad that I was going back to my room to revise. Which I did. But only after I'd found the jumper that Ella had mentioned.

*   *   *

By five thirty, I'd had enough of my studying so I shut my folders and put them away. It was time for a cup of tea and another soak in the bath. Being the dutiful daughter that I am, I made tea for everyone before I slunk upstairs to pamper myself in the bubbles.

I handed Mum her tea and then I confessed (well nearly). "Er, I'm going out tonight with Ruth and some of the other girls from school." (I had my fingers crossed behind my back.) "I won't be late – we're going for a pizza in that new place in the High Street."

"But what about your revision, Cassie? You were out last night and you've not got long before the exams start, have you? I'm not sure that you should."

"Oh, Mum!" She couldn't stop me, could she? That would be too humiliating.

Fortunately, Ella helped me out. "Come on, Mum. Give Cassie a break. After all, she's been studying all of today, hasn't she? And she's got all of next week and the week after as well. It will do her good to get out and forget about the exams for a while, anyway." (Go for it, Ella, go for it.)

Mum sipped her tea and was about to come out with a reason against forgetting about exams when she stopped herself. "All right – but don't be too late."

"I won't." I zoomed up the stairs towards the bathroom before Mum could change her mind.

I listened to some music while I was in the bath and then puffed myself all over with some talc. Then I took my Discman with me back to my bedroom where I sorted out my hair and did my make-up. Ella came in when I had nearly finished and asked if there was anything she could do to help.

"I've been trying to remember all the tips you gave me yesterday. What do you think?" I flashed my newly made-up face at her.

"It looks good – but shouldn't you have put the jumper on before you did your face?"

"Oh stuff!" Trust me to think I was doing the right thing when I was actually making a big mess of it.

"Don't worry, it'll probably be OK. But if I were you I'd take the lip-gloss off with a tissue before you put the jumper on and then reapply it afterwards," Ella laughed.

A few minutes later, I'd got the jumper on and had re-done the gloss. I put on my jeans and decided to wear my trainers instead of my Roos look-alikes – I didn't really fancy falling flat on my face into a pizza.

"So, how do I look?"

Ella gave me the once-over. "Not bad. Not bad at all."

"Not bad but not exactly good, you mean?" I was easily offended these days.

"God – I sound like Mum. Listen, you look great," Ella laughed and made me laugh with her. "Remember that time when you didn't get the top mark in your ballet exam and Mum went berserk?"

"Oh yes," I said as I rebrushed my hair. "And I said, 'Well, I wanted an award badge in a different colour for a change.' "

The pair of us giggled like idiots and started to rabbit on for ages about all the silly things we'd got up to when I was much younger and Ella was in her early teens. It was the first time we'd been able to laugh about how we'd successfully wound each other up when Ella had been living at home.

I looked at my watch. It was twenty-five to seven. So I gave myself a quick spritz of perfume and grabbed my jacket and purse. I said my goodbyes to Ella and to Mum and Dad and listened to all the dire warnings about making sure I didn't walk home on my own, and did I have my phonecard with me, and stuff. Actually, Dad did give me some money to contribute to my evening out, so it wasn't all that bad.

At the end of my street, I got a mirror out of my Prada bag and, under a street lamp, applied a deep red, fake glass Bindi to my forehead. If it was good enough for Kate Forcet (the model) then it was good enough for me. And Tom.

Sam and Ben were both at home watching the Sunday sports programme on the telly when I knocked for Ruth and Greg.

"You look good, Cassie," Sam said as I sat down to wait with Greg while Ruth went to the loo. "Where are you off to tonight?"

"Pizza-the-Action. Ever been there?"

"Not yet – you'll have to let me know if it's any good. Hey, here comes our little sister."

Ruth came into the room wearing her new silver skiing jacket. She looked terrific in it. "Cass, hi there. Love your jumper. Great Bindi, too. You guys ready? Let's get going, then."

There was never any messing with Ruth.

Tom wasn't at the restaurant when we arrived but we sat down at a table in the window and ordered something to drink while we waited for him. I was idly reading the menu and Ruth and Greg were chatting about life when there was a roar outside followed by "da da dada dada dada da da da da". Tom had arrived.

We watched him park, right outside the pizza place, and then he rushed in and greeted me as enthusiastically as he had outside Tiffany's house.

"Cassie, my gorgeous one!" I seemed to be encased in Tom and when I finally managed to release myself from his grip, I noticed that the other people in the restaurant were staring at us. Yes, that's right, I started to blush.

"So, what's on the menu, apart from you, Cassie?"

Ruth just looked at Tom in disbelief. Tom put a mobile phone down on the table (good grief, he had one already?) and Greg sunk lower into his chair and tried to cover up his face with the menu.

Fortunately, there wasn't any time for us to answer Tom before the waitress came along.

"Are you ready to order?"

We were and while we waited for the pizzas to be cooked we chatted about Tiffany's house and the party the night before.

"So whereabouts do you live, Tom?" Ruth was in her usual forthright mood. And thank goodness – because I hadn't got round to asking Tom that myself yet.

"Oh, over by the park. You know, one of the big houses overlooking the park. My grandparents used to own it and my parents moved in just after I was born. It's great, we've got a live-in housekeeper who looks after everything for us. And she lives there when we go off to the house in France every summer and when we go skiing."

There wasn't much you could say to that really. I began to think he was a bit of a berk and looked over to Ruth and rolled my eyes. But Tom didn't seem to notice and just went on and on about how his dad owned his own chain of hotels. He didn't mention what his mum did for a living – perhaps she didn't work. We heard how Tom had a sister who was away at boarding school and that when he'd been to university he wanted to help his dad to set up a chain of health spas. Fortunately, Tom spoke so much that I didn't have to think up too many things to say. It was beginning to seem just like it was at Tiffany's party.

Our pizzas arrived and it was only when I started to cut into mine that I realised what a mistake it was to have chosen a pizza that had four different cheeses on it. Every time I lifted my fork, great elastic pieces of cheese moved from my plate to my mouth – and didn't snap. I don't suppose the Sisters Cool have this problem, do you? As I wrestled with my spaghetti-like pizza, the others tucked into their food too. Tom had chosen a pizza with an egg and spinach on top and he didn't seem to notice that he'd got a great slop of egg down his front. Should I say something? I looked at Ruth and nodded in the direction of the egg. At first she didn't seem to know what I was on about but then she twigged – and she started to giggle. Greg and Tom just looked at her.

"What's the joke, Ruth?" Tom asked, eager to join in the laughter.

"Sorry, Tom – you've spilled something down your front." Ruth picked up her napkin and tried to stifle her giggles with it. Which started me off too.

Tom started wiping away – clearly he felt a bit uncomfortable and I began to feel a bit mean.

"So, Tom," Greg said, "are you coming to the match in

Bath next week? I gather the coach has organised a bus to take us there."

"You bet. Last time the college team played the Bath one we beat them hollow. So I want to do my bit for the team this time. You going too?"

And then Tom started another long conversation about his skills on the basketball court. Every now and then, Ruth and I tried to join in the chat or tried to strike up a conversation about something we were interested in. Greg seemed quite happy to talk but Tom seemed only to be interested in himself. It was a relief for us girls when the pudding we'd chosen arrived.

I tucked into my meringue only to find it wasn't quite as hard as I had expected. My spoon sliced through the meringue, crushing it and sending splinters of sugary confection in all directions across the table. Now it was Tom's turn to laugh.

"Steady on, Cassie – there's no need to get that excited about it!"

"Sorry." I started to pick up the bits of meringue which were spread everywhere but there were so many I just stopped. I put my spoon down and gave up on dessert. I was blushing so furiously I could feel myself melt. I put my hand up to my forehead – which was when I knocked my Bindi off and it fell with a tinkle on to my plate. It probably wouldn't have been so bad if the Bindi had just landed and stopped. But it didn't. Instead it bounced from my plate, then twice across the table towards Tom's plate. Tom put his hand out and caught it.

"Howzat!" He was clearly very pleased with himself. Tom handed the Bindi back to me. "Better keep an eye on this," he said, plonking it back into my hand.

I looked at Ruth as if I was pleading for mercy. Surely I was going to die. I hoped she was a good mind reader because all I wanted to do now was go home. A date surely had to be better than this?

Fortunately, Ruth picked up on my problem.

"Well, that was great but I'd better be getting back home." Ruth called the waitress over and asked for the bill.

"Yes, I'd better be going too," I said. "I've got loads of revision to do in the morning."

Greg divided the bill between the four of us and we all got out our cash – except for Tom, that is, who suddenly realised he hadn't got any cash on him. To be fair, I don't think that Tom did it on purpose but it did seem to be a fitting way for him to finish the evening. So Greg redivided the money again into three and Tom promised to pay us all back next week. Ella wouldn't believe this story in the morning!

Once the money was sorted we drifted out of the pizza place and stood in an awkward jumble on the pavement.

"Can I at least offer you guys a lift home?"

Before we could reply, Tom had opened his car and was ushering us into the seats. This time, Ruth and Greg were dropped off at Ruth's house first and then Tom parked at the corner of my road. At first I couldn't understand why he wasn't pulling up outside my house, but then I realised why when he switched off the engine and lunged towards me, pinning me against the seat. This was it! The snog situation!

As Tom's face got closer to mine, he said, "So, Cassie," which was when I spotted the spinach stuck to one of his top teeth. Gross!

I was pinned so successfully that I couldn't escape – but I could move my head round towards the window. Which is what I did, making our noses crash into each other. Tom pulled back a bit and gave a deep sigh. And that was when I realised his breath wasn't that fresh either. At least I assumed it was his breath and not mine. I'd never read about this situation in *Girl Power*. There had never been a bloke with bad breath and spinach on his teeth.

"Well, thanks, Tom. I'd better get going." I pushed him away – quite hard – and fumbled for the door handle. I found it and opened it. The fresh cool night air flooded into the car like a relief. "Well, perhaps I'll give you a call after I've done my exams. I won't have much time before then." As excuses went, it was pathetic but I think there was no doubt that Tom had now got the hint.

"Yes, see you some time, Cassie. Night."

Clutching my Prada bag, I ran up the road to home – at least this time my mum wasn't standing with the door open. Once I was inside, I checked myself in the hall mirror before I went into the living-room. I couldn't see any evidence of being mauled by Tom but I patted my hair a bit and went in.

"Hi, folks," I said and sat down on the sofa.

"Hello, Cassie," Mum said, glancing up from the video they were all watching. "Did you have a good time?"

Oh boy, Mother, if you only knew . . .

HAVE BEENS, COULD HAVE BEENS AND NEVER WERES

Tuesday morning was completely mad in our house. Mum was flapping about all over the place because today was the big day for Ella: she had to go along for her "look-see" with the cosmetic company. Dad had already left for work by the time I emerged from my bedroom – but Mum was in such a state that I began to wonder if Dad had actually run away from home. Normally, Ella is quite a laid-back person herself but today even she was tense. She'd already got her portfolio of pictures ready by the door along with a huge black bag that seemed to be stuffed with things. Goodness knows what was in the bag. At one point I dared to ask but Ella just snapped at me "It's all my kit" so I slunk into the kitchen to get my breakfast and stayed there in peace.

At about nine o'clock, a chauffeur-driven car arrived to collect Ella and take her to the photographer's studio in London where Ella was going to meet the big boss from the cosmetic company. Apparently they wanted to make sure she got there without the inconvenience of public transport. I popped out of the kitchen and wished her luck – Mum, on the other hand, couldn't resist going out to the car with Ella and giving her a dramatic kiss before she waved for about half an hour at the end of the path. Honestly, the car must have arrived at the studio before she stopped waving goodbye.

I was sitting in the kitchen contemplating my fate when Mum came back into the house and started to tidy everything up. As she vacuumed, I sat and wondered why it was that my relationships with boys seemed to be completely doomed. Neither of my dates with Tom had gone the way they should have done: there was no mention in any of the magazine articles I'd read about boys not being any better at dates than girls. Every film or telly programme I'd seen about boy-meets-girl, girl-and-boy-have-a-hot-date had made it clear that it had been a good experience. There was no elastic cheesy pizza. No turning up at parties without being invited. And certainly no spinach on smelly teeth.

I was beginning to feel seriously sorry for myself when

the phone rang. Mum didn't hear it because she was still busy with her vacuuming so I answered it.

"Hello?"

"Cassie, it's Ruth. How are you?" She sounded dramatic.

"Oh, OK, I suppose," I sighed and hoped I sounded equally as dramatic as Ruth.

"So what happened with Tom, then?"

"Too much – and not enough, really." Could I tell even my best mate that my first snog was ruined? Wasn't that like admitting in public that you were a complete failure as far as boys were concerned?

"What are you talking about? So what happened?" Ruth was not going to give up on me.

Fortunately, my mum started to vacuum the stairs at that very moment. She was oblivious to the fact that I was chatting on the phone. But Ruth could hear her loud and clear.

"Is that your mum brandishing her vacuum cleaner again? Listen, you fancy going for a walk in the park later?"

"Well, I really ought to do some revision." The noise of the vacuum cleaner was getting louder and closer to the phone.

"OK, well do that. But come round and pick me up at about twelve thirty. I'll make us some sandwiches and we can have a bit of a picnic lunch."

"OK." Mum was almost vacuuming me and the phone by now. "I'll see you then!" I shouted and put down the receiver.

Mum bumped into me as she got to the bottom of the stairs.

"Oh, Cassie, I'm sorry. I didn't see you there. I was thinking about Ella." She turned the vaccuum cleaner off and started to wind its flex round the handle. "So what are you up to today?"

"Oh, some revision. Then I'm going to meet Ruth for a picnic lunch in the park. And then – more revision. You know, life is so exciting, these days." I was playing with my zit with my fingers.

"Never mind. It won't be for long. The exams don't last for ever – and then you'll have the entire extra-long post-exam summer holidays to have fun."

Yes, and without a boyfriend, I thought.

My face obviously looked as dreary as I felt because Mum stroked me on the cheek and said, "Cheer up, sweetheart. It may never happen." (It already has! I wanted to scream.) "Shall I bring you up some coffee in about half an hour or so? Just before I go off to the studio?"

I nodded my head. "Yes, thanks. That would be nice. See you in a bit, then." And I slunk upstairs to start on my Human Biology revision.

*　*　*

I found it really hard to concentrate on my work that morning so I was bang on time going round to Ruth's. Unusually, her house was empty – not even her brothers were in. Ruth grabbed a carrier bag and stuffed the sandwiches she had made into it.

"I thought we could get a drink in the park," she said. "Come on, let's get into the sunshine and we'll see if we can make you feel better."

On the short walk to the park, we talked about Tom and the two dates.

"He wasn't anything like I thought he'd be. So much for being the prince in my fairy story. He wasn't even very cool – even though he is good-looking. OK, I'll give him that – he was at least the handsome part of the prince bit." I had my hands stuffed into my jacket pockets and I was looking down at the pavement as we walked along.

"Yeah . . ." Ruth didn't seem to know what to say. "Listen, Cass, are you going to see him again?"

"No, I don't think so. To be honest, even if he did ask me out again, I don't think I'd go. I mean, do I need a boy so desperately that I'd go out with one that's got egg on his sweatshirt?"

Ruth started to laugh. "He was a bit of a plonker, wasn't he?"

Her laugh was, as usual, infectious and I couldn't help

myself joining in. "I know. And as for his car! I'm surprised he didn't have a gold medallion on."

"And furry dice hanging down the windscreen!" Ruth put her arm round me and gave me one of her bear hugs.

"But what am I going to do, Ruth? I'm sixteen in a month's time and I still haven't got a boyfriend!" I sounded as desperate as I felt.

"So what, Cassie?"

"So you have, Ruth! You've got the gorgeous Greg. He's good-looking, good company and, well, good fun, isn't he?" She didn't know how lucky she was.

"Yes, I suppose he is. But I don't want to spend all my time with him. And anyway, I didn't set out to find him, he just came along."

"Huh." I dug my hands deeper into my pockets as we turned into the gates of the park. So why hadn't he, or at least someone like him just come along to me? We walked silently towards the centre of the park before we got to the refreshment hut. I bought us two cans of drink and then we went off to find a bench.

"Look, Ruth. Isn't that Sam and Ben over there?" I pointed over to a football game about twenty metres away.

"Oh yeah." Ruth didn't seem that surprised to find them there. "Let's sit here and we can watch them if you like."

"OK."

We sat down and tucked into our sandwiches. Ruth

had made some good ones – tuna with onion and cheese and tomato. Scrummy. We munched away and talked about the ever-fascinating subject of boys – occasionally using the ones playing five-a-side football with Sam and Ben as examples of our desperation with the male species.

"I mean, look at that one in Ben's team." Ruth pointed to a boy with red hair. "He's got a bum like a bus." We laughed.

"And how about the one in Sam's team wearing his sunglasses. It's not even that sunny today. Posy or what?"

"Phew!" Ruth exclaimed. "I can't tell you how good it is to hear you sounding more like your old self. You know – fun. Jokey."

"Fun? Me?" I'd never thought of myself as fun before. Wasn't I plain old ordinary Cassie Lang who had the sister who was fun and gorgeous?

"Yes, you are. Just relax about life a bit more. You know, real life isn't exactly like it is in the magazines. It's not a fairy story with handsome princes and lots of parties and pretty frocks. There's more than one frog out there that you've got to kiss. And even then, your prince may not be that charming."

We giggled again and carried on watching the game. Ruth started to cheer on Ben's team who were winning so it only seemed fair for me to support Sam's team. Towards the end of the game, the score could have gone either way and it was getting quite exciting. But in the end, Sam scored the winning goal.

The players strolled away from the pitch and chatted amongst themselves while they put their tracksuits on. Sam came over towards us.

"Hi, you two. I didn't know you were going to come and cheer us on."

"Neither did we." I smiled at Sam. "Well done – great goal."

"Thanks, Cass," Sam smiled back. "So what are you two doing today, then?"

"Oh, you know. Talking about lipstick and boys, a bit of revision. The usual sort of thing," I replied.

Sam laughed. "I'm glad to see you're having more fun than you seemed to have on Saturday night. I gather Tom wasn't much of a success."

"You could say that. I think I should have realised when I saw his car."

"I only wish I'd known he had it – then I could have warned you. But I think it's new. He's certainly never taken it to college."

"Oh well, it doesn't matter really."

Ruth had wandered over to chat with some of the others. Someone had obviously just told a joke because they all started to laugh.

"I wish I was as good at life as Ruth," I sighed and kicked at a tuft of grass.

"What do you mean?" Sam gave me a funny look.

"You know, getting on with people and stuff."

"You do too, you know." Sam was doing up his trainers.

"Do what?"

"Get on with people. You're getting on with me, aren't you?" Sam smiled again.

"Well . . . yes." I supposed I did if I thought about it.

"In fact, I was wondering if you'd come with me to see that new film at the Ritzy on Friday." Sam stood up from tying his laces and looked straight at me.

"Who, me? Go out with you?" Surely I hadn't heard him properly.

"What, am I that bad? I know I'm only Ruth's brother and that you've known me for ever but . . ."

"Sorry, Sam – I didn't mean that!" I blushed furiously. Some things never change!

"So? Do you fancy coming or not?"

"Er, yes, I suppose so." Did he mean on our own? I wondered. On a date?

"Well, I'll pick you up on Friday night, then. OK?"

"Yes, OK. I mean, that would be great, I'll look forward to it." I found myself grinning like an idiot.

Ruth came back over towards us with the rest of the crowd. "We're going to go to the park café for a coffee.

You two fancy joining us?"

"Yes." We both said it in unison and set off behind the others.

Sam walked a bit ahead of me and I took the chance to have a look at the way he walked. He didn't seem to hop or bounce. Was he a frog or a toad?

I went home in the early afternoon feeling guilty that I hadn't done any more revision. But even when I started to work, I was too busy thinking about what had happened earlier in the day. Had I really had a normal conversation with a boy? Had Sam really asked me out for a date?

I rang Ruth and asked her if she thought it was true.

"Course it is! Sam's fancied you for ages, dumbo."

"You're kidding!" I couldn't believe it.

Just then, a cab pulled up outside. It was Ella back from her cosmetic company.

"Look, Ruth, Ella's just got back from her thing. I'll call you later. Bye."

Mum wasn't back from the studio yet so I opened the door to let Ella in. It was obvious from the enormous grin she had on her face that she'd got the job.

"They were great. I'm going to be their Face of the Year – and I'll get loads of free make-up and perfume." Ella was thrilled. I was thrilled for her too. She told me every-thing while we sat in the living-room going through some of the goodies that they'd given her to take away with her. She was going to be coming back to London quite often during the year so I'd see a lot more of her again. Once upon a time, I wouldn't have been that bothered. But now I was glad – after all, we seemed to be friends these days.

When I'd heard all of Ella's news, I told her about Sam asking me out.

"Oh that's great, Cassie. He always seemed really nice." Ella squirted herself and me with one of the perfumes she'd been given.

"You know, I think he is."

"So there is life after Tom?" Ella smiled.

"Yep. I think Tom is one of life's toads."

"A toad?" Ella looked surprised.

"You know, instead of a frog that turns out to be a handsome prince. Don't worry, it's a private joke between Ruth and me."

"Oh, I see." Ella started to tidy up her booty. After all, Mum would be home soon and she'd throw a wobbly if the house was messed up.

I sat back on the sofa and contemplated the last few days. Perhaps reality wasn't so bad after all.